# *At Tildy's Thrift*

Also by Eulie Rier Cienfuegos

*Budding in Southern Exposure*

# *At Tildy's Thrift*

*Eulie Rier Cienfuegos*

WESTBOW
PRESS
A DIVISION OF THOMAS NELSON

WestBow Press books may be ordered through booksellers or by contacting:

WestBow Press
A Division of Thomas Nelson
1663 Liberty Drive
Bloomington, IN 47403
www.westbowpress.com
1-(866) 928-1240

ISBN: 978-1-4497-2477-1 (sc)
ISBN: 978-1-4497-2476-4 (hc)
ISBN: 978-1-4497-2475-7 (e)

Library of Congress Control Number: 2012900819

Printed in the United States of America

WestBow Press rev. date: 1/17/2012

To the Appalachian citizenry whose culture refreshes and enriches the United States.

To my daughter, Gwenith, who lived in Charleston at a young age and began to speak in the picturesque language of the people of the Low Country; and to my daughter, Rovena, who was born in that beautiful city.

To Harvey, my love and my inspiration.

*Everything done in darkness will come to light.*
(Mark 4:22 NKJV)

# ॐ Author's Note

I really enjoyed writing this book, and I sincerely hope you enjoy reading it. I lived and taught school in Charleston, South Carolina, and I never forgot the interesting culture of that city. When I taught there, as well as in the District of Columbia and in San Diego, I developed and used the procedure in the following text to address bullying and cruel teasing, behaviors all too prevalent today.

"In the Gloaming," a song that is important to two characters in the book, was copyrighted in 1881 by Annie F. Harrison, an Irish woman, and is now in public domain. It is very sentimental, and we sang it at our elementary school. The words always brought a tear to my eyes, and the music had just the right chords to tear at my heartstrings.

The folksy philosophies and speech of Tildy's clients are reminiscent of the people of the Appalachian and Low Country areas, although they do not represent any person or persons I have known.

A thrift store has customers of every type, and Tildy's clients run the gamut. People are usually looking for something special, checking out bargains, or hoping to find and purchase unusual items, while also exploring vintage antiques. The colorful (and often the strange) shop there even though Tildy's is said to be haunted. The gospel-singing trio that works in the donation intake room creates a special atmosphere, but there also lurks one who wants to destroy the shop because of a longstanding personal grievance.

At Tildy's, anything is apt to happen, and it does indeed.

# ꙅ Acknowledgements

Thanks to all of my friends who enjoyed reading about Hortonville in *Budding in Southern Exposure* and encouraged me to revisit the little Southern town, so here is *At Tildy's Thrift.*

Thanks also to the lovely hospitable people of South Carolina's Low Country. I apologize if I didn't get the language just right.

Jim Ross, who volunteers at a local thrift shop, offered me many helpful ideas, and my friend, Betty Plumbley of the California Writers Group, read some of the manuscript and encouraged me to continue, as did my wonderful art teacher, Connie Ward, and many members of Apple Valley Church of the Nazarene, who were so enthusiastic about my first book.

I really appreciate the expert editorial work of Westbow's staff, who pointed out things I hadn't noticed in the original manuscript.

# Chapter 1

As she walked to the door of her business--Tildy's Thrift Shop--, Matilda noticed Miss Maxie securing her "buggy" to a nearby telephone pole. Her buggy was a creaking old bicycle with a lawnmower-clippings bag that had been converted into an overhead shade held up by PVC pipes that were well secured to the back and sides of the bicycle. There she tied her plastic-bagged purchases after filling the small wire basket attached to the front. It wasn't the loveliest contraption, but it served its purposes. A real seventy-eight-year-old eccentric, she was going toward the store when Jerlene, the slender middle-aged sales clerk, was also just coming from the parking lot.

"How are you doing this mornin'?" Jerlene called out to Matilda, and she nodded to Miss Maxie, who was coming in behind her, the first customer of the day.

Miss Maxie answered, "Why, just fine, just fine!" She thought the question was directed to her. "You know it's about three months till Christmas! What's come through in red sweaters? You know I have to get a fresh one every year! I must upgrade!"

"I'm doing all right, Jerlene," Matilda finally responded to Jerlene from behind the front counter.

"You know, Miss Maxie, I remember seeing a nice red sweater that was brought out just yesterday. I think it was mixed with angora, and it just might be your size. Check over there." Matilda cocked her head toward the far right area where the ladies' blouses and sweaters were displayed by color. As one of the regulars, Miss Maxie always bought something, but some people came in just to browse the new items that had recently been donated or to visit with their neighbors. Matilda was nurse, confidante, counselor, and advisor to several of her customers because she was a good listener, and some people needed a listening ear. It was seemingly in short supply these days. At least they could get a hearing at Tildy's instead of at a bar.

After Matilda readied the cash register for business, she turned and watched as Miss Maxie rifled through the rack and preened in front of a mirror. She wondered if the lady had been deprived of celebrating Christmas during her childhood since that season seemed the only time she came alive with enthusiasm. Somebody said they heard Dr. Jordan remark that she may have had an arrested childhood. Tall and thin with a long, knifelike nose, she wore an austere expression most of the time—except when she spoke of Christmas. Her face lit up like a Christmas tree when she talked about the holiday. She wore her gray hair flipped on each side, winged out like a bird in flight, and a lorgnette would have suited her face perfectly. Her old, gray-mottled stone house with ivy climbing up the sides resembled a museum, except within its rooms, all of which were decorated for Christmas year-long. Matilda wondered whether Miss Maxie had grown up without celebrating Christmas. Were her parents miserly, and was she now compensating?

She had a trace of a foreign accent. Was it German? Swiss? There were so many lovely winter scenes of Germany and Switzerland on Christmas cards that someone holding them could almost feel the frosty air and smell the pines of the *Schwarzwald* there. Wasn't "Silent Night" written by a German? Yes. His name was Gruber, she recalled. It was hard to imagine anyone from that beautiful holiday area not being entranced by Christmas.

Matilda had seen Miss Maxie's living room through her front window. It was like a winter wonderland throughout the year, filled with Santa Clauses and sleighs and reindeer of all sizes and kinds—ceramic, plaster, wooden, and plastic ones on glitzy, white flannel that appeared like snow. She even had the walls of the room painted a Christmas green and a gay candy-striped border. Teddy bears of all sizes sat on windowsills and in the corners. It was always Christmas at Miss Maxie's house.

Matilda's thoughts were interrupted when suddenly Miss Maxie chirped, "Oh, my! The partridge! I must have a partridge!" She was looking around agitatedly at the knickknack shelves. She then made her way to the donation intake room where three ladies were singing as they worked.

Magnolia feigned delight on her round caramel face when she saw her and said brightly, "Oh, how you, Miss Maxie? What can we do for you?"

"Oh, my dear! I am missing a partridge for my pear tree! Do you have one back here? I simply must have one!" She cocked her head expectantly, the wings of her hair at forty-five degrees, a bird coming in for a landing.

Vilma, a dark lady from the South Carolina Low Country with large, smiling brown eyes, looked directly at her and said in her native dialect, "Miss Maxie, I know you already got de partridge in de pear tree somewhere in your wunnerful c'llecshun!"

"I thought I did, but no, I don't. I do have a pretty red cardinal sitting on a twig in the snow, but Christmas *must* have a partridge in a pear tree. I've made lords a-leaping out of pipe cleaners, and I've got swans a-swimming already. Well, save one for me if any come in—would you please?" she chirped as she twittered out to pay for her red sweater.

"Sure we will, Miss Maxie. We'll be sure to save it," said freckled Annelise.

# ❦ Chapter 2

Faint harmonic sounds were coming from the back already this morning. It was 8:30, and the three ladies who handled the donations were tuning up. In the front of the shop, Matilda and Jerlene listened to the pleasant blended sounds of their song.

*One of these mornings bright and fair,*
*Gonna take my wings and just cleave the air.*
*When I get to heaven, gonna sing and shout!*
*Ain't nobody there is gonna turn me out!*

Matilda smiled and fingered a curl at the side of her neck. She'd learned some of their songs herself, the ones they sang most often. This old spiritual was one of them. She hummed along at the cashier's desk. She loved these old ladies, and today she recalled when and where they had met three years before. It was at a Labor Day event when people from all over Hortonville came together for a picnic at Salyers Park and Field, named in honor of the deceased Judge Owen Salyers. The function was organized to promote the spirit of brotherhood as well as to celebrate the working man.

Checkered tablecloths and a variegated panorama of blankets were spread on the ground for seating and placement of the sumptuous fare of fried chicken, spicy pork barbecue, hot chili, potato salad, sweet apple pie, peach cobbler, and homemade ice cream. Businessmen were there to network and publicize their services and materials. Congregations from Charity Catholic Church in midtown, Crestview United Church of prestigious Oak Heights high up on the hill, First True Delivered and New Dawn Community Churches in the minority community of Beantown were all well represented and were evangelizing and enjoying fellowship. Freeloaders had come just to sample the fare. Some spinsters and bachelors were there to survey the crowd, seeking those who were eligible for relationships. Teenagers came to eat the homemade ice cream, pies, and desserts and to check out the opposite sex while giggling, flirting, flexing muscles, showing off in games, teasing, and sometimes just proving to be a nuisance. Everyone had looked forward to this special occasion on the plush grassy area next to the baseball diamond of Judge Salyers Field, and the weather was cooperating nicely enough for them to even play a game of baseball.

A wooden stage with amplification was set up for people to speak or to perform if they desired. Matilda noticed a trio of women dressed in black and white walking onto the stage. The plump one with a cheerful caramel face and curly pressed hair introduced herself as Magnolia Washington. A second lady had an accent and introduced herself as Vilma Jeanmarie. She was thin with dark chocolate skin and had thickly braided, salt and pepper hair. The third lady was slender with a freckled light complexion and a cloud of coarse reddish hair. She introduced herself as Annelise Harris. Magnolia, apparently the spokesperson, announced that they were the Harmonettes from First True Delivered Church in Beantown. Then they began to tune up and sing in such rich sonorous harmony that many picnickers stopped eating and took notice.

*We're workin' on a building with a true foundation,*
*Holdin' up the bloodstained banner of the Lord.*
*We never get tired of workin' on the building.*
*We're goin' up to heaven to get our reward.*

During the feasting and congeniality that followed, Matilda sought out these ladies to tell them how much she had enjoyed their singing.

"How y'all ladies doin'?" she said brightly. "I sure did enjoy your singin'."

"Fine. We just fine. Thank you."

"Who you?" This from the dark, thin one, peering closely.

"I'm Matilda Dayton, and I own Tildy's Thrift Shop. Y'all come in sometime. I'm in the green and white building on the corner of Oak and Baker. Come to think of it, I could use some help in the donations room, if y'all know anybody who's interested."

All three ladies had been interested, and now they were working together at Tildy's, taking in donations and sorting used clothing according to sex, size, and condition, as well as linens, shoes, working electronics, toys, hardware, etc. They worked at a long table opening bags and boxes. A large can sat on the floor at each end of the table for depositing soiled and unusable items. Those in need of minor mending were put in a separate pile. These would be taken home by the ladies. They would be mended, cleaned, and given to the needy of the community instead of being thrown away. The electrical items were handed over to Chester Weems, the forty-year-old widowed custodian and electrician, whose workbench was in the far corner of the same room.

The best and least used donations of clothing, furniture, and electronics came from the Economic Development Corporation, headed by Mrs. Pauline Hardee, her husband, Barney, and composed of other professionals who had moved into the area. The corporation had ventured capital for Matilda to purchase the building for Tildy's Thrift.

Magnolia Washington was the leader of the trio. She was a feisty fifth-generation Beantown resident. She and her younger siblings had been reared by their mother and grandmother.

Her father had enlisted in the Army in World War II, and was stationed in Paris, France. Enthralled with the freedom he experienced there as a black man, he went AWOL rather than returning to the racial codes of rural Virginia. He wrote to his family and said he was saving money to bring them to France too, but the letters finally stopped, and he was never heard from again.

After her grandmother died and her mother became too ill to do domestic work in the homes of Oak Heights, Magnolia stopped school in the tenth grade and began to work as a domestic in order to support the family. Her siblings had finished high school, were now married, and lived in cities further north.

She had married late in life. Her husband, Roy, retired from the coal mines after he contracted silicosis, but he did what he could to help around the house. She loved him and always tried to find something he could help her with in order to build up his pride.

Now, she stuck her head into the other room and greeted the ladies in the front office.

"How y'all doin' this mornin', Tildy? Jerlene?"

"Oh, fine, 'Nolia. Y'all okay?" they answered.

"Oh yes, no new mis'ries to speak of 'cept a tetch of arthritis in my hip, Tildy," Magnolia said.

The other two ladies agreed that they were doing "fair to middlin" and went about their tasks of pulling articles from bags and boxes.

Annelise clucked her tongue and remarked that somebody had surely mixed up their trash bags with their donation bags this morning after she emptied a bag on the table and several dead roaches fell out with a lot of dried red rose petals. When a dead rat in a trap also fell out, she felt sick and had to leave the area. Luckily the ladies used latex gloves, but they were aghast at this. Matilda wondered if it was some kind of prank. Chester, the custodian, cleaned up their area, but the ladies had to take the rest of the day off. Matilda said she understood. The next day they were still talking about the filthy bag, and they were careful when pulling out items.

When Magnolia put a closed box on the table and started to open it, Vilma said, "Keerful, 'Nolia. Might be somet'ing live in 'ere for true!"

Magnolia said, "It don't wanna tangle with me. I got this flatiron over here." She pointed to an ancient one someone had donated.

Vilma laughed, but she said, "Flatiron don't kill ghostsies. You know one is s'pose to be in this here place. De ghost of that dead pusson long time ago."

"What? A person died in here?" Annelise asked.

Vilma then began to tell them about rumors she had heard in the community—that the dead body of a young woman had been found in this building about ten years ago. Even Chester was wide-eyed as she talked.

She said, "I know there be hants for true too. One day I'll tell y'all 'bout da boo hag!"

Vilma hailed from John's Island, known as geechie country near Charleston, South Carolina. The people there spoke the African-Anglicized Gullah tongue that came from the slave ancestors of Angola. On John's Island, her aged father still served as a griot—one of the respected elders who recited the history of the forefathers by oral tradition. She recalled her last sight of him—a small, wrinkled, dark prune of a man who seemed to be holding court with a group of young people sitting enthralled at his feet.

She had told Matilda how proud she felt when she too sat enthralled at his feet as he transmitted the story of his great-grandfather who was born in slavery in the West Indies. It was July 31, 1834 when this ancestor, along with a small group of male slaves, stayed up all night to see the dawning of August 1, the day they would be free men, no longer legally enslaved, no longer property, but recognized as free human beings. As the sun rose in the east, they breathed heavily, smelling Freedom Day. Some cried for joy, and others shouted hallelujahs. A few laughed and found it hard to stop. They had been reborn! The children and the women caught the emotion of the men and cried as well.

Vilma had once been married to a man from the mainland, whose business was selling Low Country crafts in the area of mossy oaks and palmettos along Charleston's Ashley River. The tourists were very much taken with the sweet grass baskets woven in the African tradition and paid handsomely for them. Sweet grass baskets had been woven in coils by slaves who gathered the long-stemmed bulrush grass from marshes and ocean fronts. The sharpened end of a spoon was used as a needle to draw in filaments of other natural fibers. The baskets were also used as fanners to separate the rice from the chaff. Vilma and the other women in their area made beautiful ones. After her husband succumbed to pneumonia in the third year of their marriage, Vilma had ventured into the Virginia area with a cousin, who had since died. Hoping she could start a basketry business, she soon found that she could not because there were no strong grasses with which to weave, coil, and plait, but she had found wonderful friends and a strong church family.

Annelise hailed from North Carolina. She was the offspring of parents in the Blue Vein Society. This was a pretentious group of mixed race persons whose veins could be seen as blue because they had light skin. In her last year of high school, she had gone to the color-line cotillion for a gala "coming out." The escorts for the event had to be blue-veined also. It was known that if a child were to date below their color, they could be disowned. A child who was a darker genetic throwback was sometimes sent north to live with a relative and certainly did not appear in the family portrait. Parents bought homes in areas where color was a consideration at the schools, so that when dating began, problems would not arise. It was known that a comb was still mounted above the doorway at a local church and that if the hair did not easily slide through that comb during Reconstruction days, the person of color could not enter.

When Annelise became a Christian in truth, she rejected this snobbishness among her people and even sought out those of darker hue for friendship. She had never married because she discovered that so many young men only looked on the outside and never appreciated her for her character or personality. She didn't want to be arm candy or eye candy for any of them. She became disenchanted with the college she attended because one of the sororities was also color-struck, and the girls chosen for favorable positions, such as Homecoming Queen, were always those with light skin and naturally straight or chemically straightened hair. So she left college after her second year and took a business course at a trade school. She had learned that this kind of separatist behavior came from the legacy of the letters sent out to slave masters in 1712 by Willie Lynch, a British plantation owner, on how to deal with slaves—how to foment jealousy and division within slave groups. Skin color, hair texture, and ways to promote feelings of dominance by female slaves over males—psychological emasculation—would be transmitted throughout the generations. Annelise found that this was still going on, not only in the South, but in other parts of the country as well. She rebelled against this attitude wherever she found it.

The fall sun slanted golden spokes through the window of the room as the ladies hummed and worked. Magnolia noticed diminutive Hector Morales one of the regular customers. He had stuck his round face with twinkling blue eyes in the doorway of the workroom. White tufts of hair had escaped from his hound's-tooth cabby cap, and he wore his customary checkered jacket.

"How's it going?" he drawled. His small-mustached mouth slit to show a bright smile.

"Hello, Hector! Thing's fine in here. How you doin'?"

"Uh, okay I guess." He stopped, as if to remember something, turning his eyes upwards and then hitting the side of his temple to jog his memory. "Oh, I know what I need! Any horseshoes come in today?"

"Don't have any just yet, Hector, but we'll set one by for you if one does come in," Annelise answered.

Hector said, "I b'lieve my luck gonna change when I get me a horseshoe nailed 'bove my front door." He smiled even more broadly.

"If destructionment come, shoe can't kick it," Vilma said with a frown on her brow.

"You ol' pagan!" Magnolia scolded. "You say you a Christian, and here you be talkin' 'bout luck! Ain't no sich a thang! There's blessin's and curses! That's all!" She looked up to the ceiling and said, "Whip that old devil outa him, Lord! Whip him!"

Hector grinned and then pulled his head back from the door sheepishly. He knew Magnolia liked to chide him. It didn't mean a thing to him; he told her he was Catholic.

# ℘ Chapter 3

Luna Carter was a petite spinster of forty-three. She had an auburn cascade of curly hair that framed a pretty oval face. Her intelligent hazel and green-flecked eyes usually seemed to be brooding over a matter. By nature, she was an academician with an inquiring mind. To her, the natural, created world was filled with wonder, and to make it her own, she enjoyed capturing scenes in a sketchbook as she sat behind her little cottage. Each natural sketch also had some creature of fancy lurking under a toadstool or peeking from leaves in a tree and such.

Her home, in the area known as Mossy Point in Hortonville, was located between the prestigious manicured hills of the muckety mucks known as Oak Heights and the mainly minority area of Beantown. The small, yellow-painted brick cottage was festooned with bluish-purple morning glories that crawled up to meet the green composition roof. It was quaint and surrounded by thick, dark turquoise pines that exuded a redolent freshness. Rather secluded and shady until the sun was high in the noon sky, it existed in a gloaming sort of way. She liked the word *gloaming* because it reminded her of her mother's voice when long ago she sang:

> *In the gloaming, O my darling,*
> *When the lights are dim and low,*
> *And the quiet shadows falling*
> *Softly come and softly go.*

Her voice was the only memory Luna had of her deceased mother. As she grew older, she found out what the word *gloaming* meant and found it appropriately descriptive of Hortonville, because there certainly was a "twilight" feeling to the town. Hortonville was surrounded by the Blue Ridge pine forests, so it was not possible to see the sun rise or set since the town was sunk down in a valley like it was in the bottom of a bowl. But it was still rather pretty, with its rivers and streams from the mountains that ran down through the rocks in the mountain clefts. People went to bed early and got up late if they didn't have to go to work. The first time she looked at picture books of the western states, she was amazed to see that there was so much of the sky that was apparent.

Her adopted parents, Tom and Geneva Carter, had told her about the deaths of her father and mother, which had occurred during a severe flu epidemic. The little house and its grounds had become her property when her adopted parents passed away some years prior.

One day when she was walking along the shallow banks of the Horton River, she saw a snake rising upright in the water like a wavy stick. She interpreted it as a dark omen—a sign that confirmed for her what she felt she really was—someone strange, alien.

She began to retreat down into her inner core, spiraling slowly like a spring until she felt tight and secure, safe. In this state, she dreamed of a sunlit meadow where she flitted through the sweetness of daylight, wispy as a gossamer fey creature of air and feathers. She alighted on a blade of grass, sniffed its sweetness, and slept there. She often lay dreaming in this fantasy meadow to escape the ugliness of reality.

"An offspring of the fallen ones," a fat, blue-haired old lady had whispered in a raspy voice to another wizened gray head when Luna picked up a few apples and put them in her shopping cart for purchase at Valu Market a few days prior. The fat, blue-haired old lady was looking wide-eyed at Luna's hand. She had taken off her right glove, which had gotten wet on top of the sink when she had used the ladies' room.

In the aisle, Luna slowly turned her head around, and her eyes met the woman's. She pretended her eyes were bottomless, smoldering embers beneath shadowy lashes. She wished she could snarl and scare the woman, but she decided to form a garish clown smile on purpose, fixing her lips into a malevolent rust-colored crescent moon, as if to say, "Am I really!" Wizened Gray Head made nervous, pursing fish lips, and Fat Blue Hair flared her nostrils and widened her eyes at her. The two old ones skittered away down the aisle, looking back quickly from time to time lest she was following them. Luna smirked bitterly.

She had put her gloves back on, but now she removed them again and looked afresh at the little inch-long nubbins with the tiny fingernails growing beside each of her little fingers.

Later in the day, she had gone to the library and researched references to the "the fallen ones." There she found references to a group of beings called Nephilim. According to Genesis 6, these were fallen angels who left their habitation and came to earth where they mated with earth's females, creating a hybrid race, ostensibly a satanic ploy to pollute the line through which the pure Messiah would come. Satan remembered the prophecy from Eden when God told him that One would come who would crush his head, while he would only bruise His heel. Genesis also said that the offspring of these unions were giants and mighty ones on the earth. In the Old Testament, some of these beings were said to have had extra fingers and toes. It is believed by some that this ungodly hybrid mixture in the genealogy of so many human beings at that time was the reason the earth was flooded, and that Noah was saved because the Bible says his lineage was not polluted. The Bible records that he was perfect in his lineage. But the Bible also said that as it was in the days of Noah, so would it be in the coming of the Son of Man, so these things must have infiltrated again since then. It was also

reported by Joshua and Caleb that they saw giants when they went
to spy out the land of Canaan under Moses's direction in the Book
of Numbers.

*So!* she concluded. *Now I know! I am one of the Nephilim! I'm not
mighty, but I am imperfect. I must have come from one of these hybrids
since I have these things on my hands!* She read on and discovered that
Goliath and his brothers were sons of Anak, and they were giants
with these additional digits. The Nephilim were all males, she also
learned.

*But I don't have six toes. I'm not male, and I'm not even very big. I
may be just part Nephilim. It must be a genetic throwback!* She fancied
that maybe now she could learn the piano and play it beautifully
with extra fingers. Maybe she would be a better typist! She would
manicure her little fingers and even put bright pink nail polish
on them like her other nails! She giggled at the thought of how
advantageous this could be.

*What would Nephilim eat?* she wondered. *Were they ogres like
the giant in Jack and the Beanstalk?* As she walked toward her home,
she passed a mulberry bush with a swarm of tiny furry whiteflies
around it. She had never seen such a large cloud of these before.
Involuntarily, she put her hand into the midst of them, made a fist,
and then put them into her mouth and swallowed. She gagged. *What
am I doing? What is wrong with me? Am I losing my mind?* By the time
she reached her house, her eyes were red and swollen from crying.

At home, after several cups of hot tea, she thought about her
adopted parents who had told her that she and her older sister had
been adopted at the ages of three and five respectively. It wasn't
known who had adopted the sister or where she was located.

When her parents took her to the doctor and inquired about the
extra growths on her hands, the doctor had told Tom and Geneva
Carter that the condition was called hexadactyly, and that the

location of her digits was common. Some babies were born with additional toes or even an extra digit between the fingers or toes. Although Dr. Martin said that he had not seen any of these cases, he had read about them in medical journals. Some parents had these digits tied so that they dropped off before the child grew too old. Tom and Geneva decided that she was too old to have this done now. They remembered the older sister vaguely but didn't recall whether she too had the extra little fingers. When Luna asked her mom about the sister, she was told that although she didn't know her whereabouts, she did recall that the sister had a red birthmark that looked like a star on the back of her neck, and that her name was Stella.

#

"Loony Luna! Loony Luna!" She awoke with a start, covered with perspiration as she remembered her nightmares—cruel singsong taunting by the children at the elementary school. She had been suffering nightmares about it ever since she moved back to Hortonville from Philadelphia last month, after the company she worked for following her graduation from high school went bankrupt. Throughout her early school years, she had been bullied and tormented as something of horror. She hated those little stubs that grew attached to each little finger, and she tried to keep her hands balled up, but the hated parts protruded shamelessly. The girls didn't want to touch her, thinking they would catch something, and the mean boys yelled out "Monster!" whenever she came around. The pretty and popular girl everyone clustered around was named Matilda. She was the most vicious of all, and Luna vowed to make her pay one day for the pain she inflicted on her as well as Luna's only friend, Cora, who was very dark. Anyone who was different was Matilda's apparent target.

"Loony Luna! Loony Luna!" The taunting kept going around and around in her head, becoming louder and louder. Luna's breath was coming faster and faster, and her heart was beating almost loudly, as she said to herself, "It won't be long. It won't be long. I've found you, and you will pay for starting all of the abuse! Yes, you'll pay! I've found you now after such a long time!" Her eyes glittered. "You'll regret abusing Luna!"

She licked her dry lips as she recalled what she saw two days ago. She was walking on Oak Street when she saw a woman locking the door of Tildy's Thrift around 4:30. Something about the woman's profile seemed familiar as she walked toward the parking lot to a small brown car after locking up. The woman was somewhat plump, but in Luna's imagination, another face superimposed itself on the profile. It really did look like Matilda! The hair was still blonde, although shorter and graying at the temples. It had to be her, and she was coming from a shop called Tildy's! *Is her name Matilda? Ah! That must be her store!*

Her nemesis had been found at last! Her mouth went dry. *Like snake spit,* she thought. Her eyes narrowed as she watched the woman enter her car. Then she had emitted an explosive sound, "Finally!"

# Chapter 4

Chester Weems was Tildy's custodian and electrician. The electrical donations and tools were put on his workbench in the area by the door so that he could check them out for usability with tools and a panel of outlets and electrical cords at his disposal there. He was taking a break by sitting reared back in a white plastic chair outside the room and chewing on a blade of sour grass when a shiny, new red truck pulled up. The bed of it was filled with chairs donated by Pauline Hardee's Music Conservatory. Jay, her twenty-two-year-old son, often brought a load of donations to Tildy's, and today, Darlinda Fields was sitting in the passenger seat. Chester clenched his jaw and spit into a nearby bucket. His eyes narrowed as he looked at them. Everyone knew Jay and Darlinda were an item and had been dating for nearly six months and were now engaged.

Mixed couples were not common here, but the citizens of Hortonville knew and respected the two old and established families. Darlinda's grandmother was none other than Ola Mae Fields, the owner of the Flora Rose Hotel and Boarding Home, and her parents were professionals from Hortonville who were now living in Los Angeles. Of course, everyone knew that Jay's mother was a liberal since she'd been educated up North. Jay Colby's stepfather, Barney Hardee, was from an old and established Hortonville family, and Jay's natural father had been police chief of Hortonville before he died.

Chester heard Jay say, "I'll be right back, sweetie," and saw her dimple a smile on her pretty brown face as he proceeded to unload the chairs in front of the door. Chester, who knew it was his job to do so, took the chairs inside as they were unloaded, saying nothing to Jay. When all was done, Jay said, "Thanks, Chester." Chester just grunted.

Chester and his friend Grayson were fishing the week before when they saw them—the dark girl and the white boy—coming in their direction from that spot some called Willow Glade. He got all worked up when he saw them and commented to Grayson, "Hit just ain't right. I know what my ma and pa taught me, and I ain't goin' agin' it. Ain't nat'ral. Oughta find her some nice colored boy, and that white boy sure could do better. Yeah, hit just ain't right."

Grayson told him about the time when that became lawful, citing the Loving case that went all the way to the Supreme Court when a white man and black woman from Virginia had married in the District of Columbia, but were arrested when they came back to Virginia and were living together. Virginia had a Racial Integrity Act against what was called miscegenation back in 1924.

"The judge said he would suspend the jail sentence if they left Virginia, so they did. The Supreme Court declared that miscegenation law unconstitutional, so people can now get married regardless of race. You just gotta get used to it, Chester," Grayson said.

"I don't care. I'm not gonna get used to it. People ought to stay with their own kind," Chester said.

He picked up his fishing gear and bait and secured it in the bed of his old blue Chevy truck. He didn't even get a nibble on his fishing line and was in a dark mood anyway from the conversation. Although he had the day off, he went back to Tildy's. He was always good at tinkering around and fixing things at home when his wife was alive. She'd been gone five years now, and he missed her a lot. Sometimes he pretended he was fixing an appliance for Nora. They had had no children, but her beloved cat, Fluffy Sue, a mixed angora sweetheart of a feline, was all he had left that she really loved. He protected that cat with all diligence.

He was still a healthy, good looking, suntanned forty-year-old man who had all of his sandy gray hair, but he hadn't been seriously interested in any woman since Nora died. He found that some of the spinsters and widows acted plumb silly around him. He had no problem with the three colored women who sorted, tossed away, and steamed the clean, wrinkled clothing. In fact, he rather liked their company, and sometimes he tapped his foot to their church songs. They also had a lot of wit. He could finally understand the strange speech of the one from the Carolina coast. He never offered much in conversation with them; that just wasn't his way, so he kept busy at his workbench. He took little breaks by sitting in his white plastic lawn chair outside the donation door. It still chafed him to remember the first day he sat there. An old man who was looking for the place to take his little bag of donations saw him and croaked, "Are you one of them homeless folks, or do you work here?"

It was Violet Stidham who was his greatest nuisance. She had adored him from high school days when he had played football and had been the loudest one cheering whenever he got the ball.

"Is that your brother?" someone would ask. Then she would proclaim loudly, "No! He's my *man*! Touchdown, Chester! Touchdown!" she would screech, waving a pennant.

Violet seemed to always come around when he was working on a disassembled appliance. Today, she teetered into the back entrance on stiletto heels around three o'clock. Chester was diagnosing some vacuum cleaners and radios.

"Oh, Chester, are you working hard today?

"Unh." He glanced up, noting the way her tight dress accentuated her scrawny appearance. She looked clownish to him, with her mass of red ringlets, red lipstick, and heavily rouged cheeks.

She chattered on about mundane things, but he didn't respond because he knew she'd finally talk herself out and leave if he didn't.

"Good riddance, Miss Priss," Magnolia said, once she was out of earshot. Chester smiled. He'd seen Magnolia's feistiness earlier that day when two purple-haired women had come into the shop and one said to the other, "Well, Mother Nature sure did give us a beautiful day today. It's so nice outside!"

Coming from the lavatory, Magnolia heard this, and she had stopped in mid-step—foot still up in the air—and said, "Mother Nature? Ain't no sich a thang! It's Father God! In the beginning, God!"

The women had looked at her as if she'd lost her mind. Magnolia had stomped into the intake room mumbling, "Don't know where folks come up with these fairytale notions no how!"

Then Annelise started up an old slave song:

> *I'm troubled, I'm troubled,*
> *So troubled in mind.*
> *If Jesus don't help me,*
> *I surely will die.*

Vilma and Magnolia soon joined in. Magnolia was at peace for the rest of the day.

# ❦ Chapter 5

Matilda had found a jewel in Jerlene. Whenever she was too sick to come in, she knew she could always depend on Jerlene to handle the front office just the way she would herself. Jerlene didn't know it, but she was the beneficiary of Tildy's in the event of Matilda's death. Today, Jerlene was inspecting the racks to collect the empty hangers and to hang up clothing that had fallen down. Matilda was folding domestics since it was a rainy day and business was slow.

Jerlene lived at the Flora Rose Boarding House in Beantown, owned by her good friend Ola Mae Fields. The fact that Ola Mae was a lady of color hadn't meant anything to her and her family. She'd lived there ever since she, her daughter, and her husband, now deceased, came from nearby Kentucky and found work at the Flora Rose. Since Hortonville was in a depressed area of Appalachia, jobs were hard to find. Her husband, Junior, was first hired at the Flora Rose as a handyman since Ola Mae was a widow. Later, Jerlene helped domestically. Several of the old colored folks who were Flora Rose boarders got bargains at Tildy's because they told Jerlene what to look for and "lay back" for them until they could come to shop, since their physical infirmities often held sway.

Jerlene's family was the first to integrate First True Delivered Church. Her daughter, Wilma Jo, was now married and teaching mathematics at the local high school. She and Ola Mae's daughter, Lauranne, had grown up together, and they became the best of friends. Lauranne was teaching at the elementary school. An accomplished pianist from the Hortonville Conservatory, she also directed the town's community chorus.

Both Jerlene and Matilda were civic-minded and had met at a business meeting of the Circle of Encouragement for Community

Revitalization, Inc. Jerlene and her husband, Elmer Suggs, had always faithfully attended before he died. They were there when the Circle started—during the time the white merchants who lived in Oak Heights became incensed at the efforts of the Beantown residents to revitalize their community through a buy/barter system. Since the Suggs were white, they would also attend some of the merchants' meetings and inform Ola Mae about what was going on. Now, however, the white merchants had stores in Beantown too, and they took items and produce on consignment from seamstresses, farmers, and others of the minority citizenry. Even a gifted Beantown painter had his paintings and sculpture now displayed at a gallery. His works were also on the walls of several of the prestigious Oak Heights mansions and hanging in the town hall and library. Jerlene and Matilda had seen many social changes in their lifetimes, and they were living history books, at least on the subject of Hortonville.

When Matilda approached Jerlene about helping out at Tildy's, she had readily accepted, and Ola Mae was happy for her to have this opportunity. Matilda told her that she couldn't afford much pay, but that as business at the store increased, she would give raises. They enjoyed each other's company as they worked together. Jerlene also added some nice decorating touches at the store, and she designed and mounted professional-looking price charts in each room. The motto on Tildy's display window was Gently Worn and Nearly New. Creamy lace curtains tied back on both sides graced the front window, and in the center of the windowsill rested a pot of bright red silk geraniums.

Jerlene had placed near the cash register today a collectible porcelain doll and carriage. It was a quaint and cute display. She'd found that some items placed on the counter were purchased on impulse at the last minute of a sale. She had good marketing sense and had become Tildy's best friend and confidante.

This past weekend, Matilda had contracted the flu and was home for a few days. On Thursday morning when Jerlene opened the shop, she was horrified to find the lace curtains at the window slit into ribbons and dried rose petals on the floor beneath. The distinct smell of rose perfume was detected as well. She gasped and then called out to the ladies who had come in by the side door, "'Nolia, would you and the ladies come in here?"

Jerlene notified Matilda, while the other ladies, aghast at the discovery, chattered in speculation about who could have done this and how they could have entered the shop. Only Vilma brought up the rumor about a haunting by the ghost of the unidentified body that had been found in the building long ago.

A call to the police brought Deputy Martin out to investigate. He found no forced entry or tampered lock, but he took the report anyway and photographed the area.

"Anybody you know of who has a grudge against Tildy's?" he asked.

No one responded positively. Chester had entered, and now he said, "Bet it was somebody from that new prison on the outskirts—a released druggie maybe."

The deputy checked the cash register. Nothing was out of order according to Jerlene. The safe was intact also.

"I recommend that y'all get a strong deadbolt lock anyway. They have some good ones over at Bi Rite Hardware," the deputy said. "Chester, I'm driving right past there, and I can show you which ones I recommend."

After a call to Matilda, Chester and Deputy Martin departed for the hardware store, while Jerlene took the damaged curtains down and Magnolia swept up the dried rose petals.

The curious people who came into the shop were sure to carry the news to the community.

#

Luna stood across the street in the shadows again and watched the flurry of activity—the coming and going of the deputy and Chester, and the pulling down of shredded curtains. She imagined the consternation and fear of those inside. Too bad there weren't a lot of customers to see the damage and smell the perfume.

Her roses had been gorgeous this year, and a few weeks ago she had gathered a bunch of blossoms that were nearly spent. She took them into the kitchen where she cut off the stems and immersed the heads in a pot of water. She turned the heat on, and soon the pot was boiling with the scent of roses filling the air. When the water cooled, she poured the liquid into a capped jug to let it set a day or two before siphoning some into a small atomizer.

She had said half-aloud, "Just the beginning, Miss Tildy, just the beginning! You'll see!"

Now the deed was done, and she walked on down Oak Street and smiled when she glanced back at Tildy's. It had been so easy to enter the store. There was only one person at the cash register, and she was tallying up the sale of a little pile of boys' clothing for a tall lady who was accompanied by two small and active children. She didn't see Matilda anywhere in the room, so she guessed Matilda was in the back. There was also a man busy rifling the shirt rack on the far side of the room.

She had walked over to the window with a small razor blade taken from a paper bag in her purse and, in the seeming act of adjusting the drapes of each panel, she had made many slits in the filmy fabric. Then she had quickly shaken out the dry petals from her bag onto the windowsill and had pressed one wide spray of rosewater from a small atomizer onto one of the panels before quickly exiting.

It was so easy! She felt no pang of conscience. In fact, she felt quite giddy. She smiled as she walked down the street en route to her home at Mossy Point and imagined Matilda's face as she discovered what had transpired. *Revenge is certainly sweet*, she thought. *It fact, it's quite delicious!*

# Chapter 6

Matilda had returned to the store, and she was quite concerned about what had happened the day before. The ladies in the back chattered about it nervously as they worked.

Vilma said, "Coulda been de ghost, but coulda been sompun else. A lot of de old miffs and tales got some trut' in 'em."

Annelise asked, "What myths?"

"I done mention 'bout de boo hag one time ago. 'Member?" Well, I need to tell it to you now. I know de devil is real! I seed him workin' 'ginst folks in de islands. He come in all kind a forms. Might be a boo hag 'roun' hyar!"

They hadn't heard of anything like that and were all ears as Vilma told them what all the old Sea Islanders knew and the children feared.

"Dat boo hag be a baaad evil t'ing what born wit' no skin, so mus' go use sombuddy else skin. Dat skin come off at night when she wear it out. Den she nuffin but wrinkly blue veins an' red muskles, so she go fly roun' thoo winders ontwell she fin' sombuddy to ride ontwell they lose they conshuss. Huh tek off de skin an' put it on huhsef. Den she ride off an' tek um to da boo daddy fuh him to gnaw him bones. When da skin wear out, she need annuder, so off she go to fly thoo somebody else winder, tek he skin, and tek he buddy to boo daddy. But a pusson can go 'gainst huh! Paint blue roun' da winder sill an' huh cain't git in. But ef you needs some ayuh an' has to cracks da winder a bit, put some salt an' peppah on da winder sill an' it bu'n up huh red meat so she scream and die. It be a hor'ble soun'. I done hyeered it!"

Vilma was shuddering. Obviously, she had heard this tale as a child and it still frightened her.

Magnolia shook her head and smirked. "Girl, you know that's just some old made-up story they done told you younguns so you'd behave yo'selves—something like the boogey man I heard about. Do boo hags use rose perfume?" Magnolia mocked.

"But it could be huh doin' mischief!" Vilma said.

"I know there is a very evil presence in this world," said Annelise. "You know what the Bible says: that we war against powers and principalities in other dimensions? That's why we're not supposed to play around with Ouija boards, people calling up spirits pretending to be our dead relatives, tarot cards, horoscopes, and such. We can open the door of our minds for demons of darkness to enter our lives. But you know what I do? I stake my life on what the Bible says! 'Greater is He Who is in me than he who is in the world.' We don't have to be afraid of no boo hag because the battle is the Lord's! Like He told Joshua, 'Stand still and see My salvation!'" Her face was flushed with passion.

Vilma and Magnolia had reared back wide-eyed and listened to her in silence. Finally, Magnolia said softly, "Annelise, we gonna make a preacher outa you yet!"

"But I still goan put outen a glass of cleah watah an' open da Bible," Vilma said. "Devil doan lak no cleah watah 'side God's open up book!"

# ⚶ Chapter 7

Matilda called a brief staff meeting at the end of the Wednesday workday. Everyone assembled in the used furniture room where they could sit and enjoy some freshly brewed coffee. Magnolia also shared her box of powdered donuts left over from lunch.

"Well, Jerlene, ladies, Chester …," Matilda began. "It's been a little slow this week. Some folks may be a little fearful after they heard about that incident with the curtains and the perfume, but we've got a lot of inventory, and some good donations are still coming in. We need to move items to display the new things. Any ideas?"

"What about putting some colored tags on items for half price?" Jerlene asked.

"Dey teks dem off and put on nudder. Dey slicks!" Vilma said.

"Depends on how you attach 'em," said Chester.

"What about those little tags with the string ties?"

"Maybe, Annelise, but we'd still have to close the store and do all of that in an afternoon, tying string and all," Tildy said.

"Can't we get us one of them guns?" asked Magnolia.

"Guns? What kind of gun?" asked Jerlene.

"Oh, now you cookin'!" said Chester. "I got one of them staplin' guns. You talkin' 'bout one of them?"

"I'm sho' not talkin' 'bout no bullet gun, Chester!"

Everybody laughed. It was getting late, and they all wanted to get home because the darkness came early now.

Then Matilda said, "I've got an idea! Let's just have a One-Dollar Hour—All You Can Fill in a Green Bag for One Dollar! Chester, open the door at ten minutes before 10:00 instead of 9:00 that day. Then tell the customers to pick up a green trash bag from a stack beside the door. Jerlene, please ring a bell at 11:00 for the shopping to stop, and Harmonettes, you ladies act as monitors to see that people stop shopping and line up to pay at that time. This could be good for business and also a lot of fun!" Her eyes were bright with excitement.

"Gonna be a bedlam for true too!" Vilma said ruefully.

Chester said, "Make sure no little kids come, because one of 'em might get stomped on! Some people get crazy when there's a real good sale. We've got to have a sign sayin' No Children Allowed!"

A huge sign about the Trash Bag Sale was posted in front of the store for the rest of the week. It announced that the event was scheduled for the following Saturday morning. At 9:30 that morning, people were lined up for half a block before the store opened at 10:00, and they were still coming. The staff inside the store was excited as they peeked out the windows and did last-minute checking inside.

Finally, the doors were opened and the shopping hour began. The frenzied customers breezed around, their green bags making parachutes as they flitted from area to area.

"I'm gettin' all the tools that'll go in this bag! This here is a real good deal!" said one man with a bottom lip full of snuff.

Jerlene touched his shoulder and pointed toward the sign near the door that read No Spittin and No Cussin. He sucked at his lip more vigorously.

"Ooh, I hope they haven't sold that skirt I wanted last week," an acne-faced teenage girl fretted.

"Hoo, boy! This is a good deal hyar!" said a white-bearded gentleman. "Look at these ties—real silk! I'm a-gittin' all o' these!"

"Will you git outta my way, puhleeze?" a heavyset woman said in exasperation to another hefty one who glared at her.

"I got some English Staffordshire saucers here, girl! They be 'spensive!" a spindly woman chirped to her friend.

"Hey! This here dress, hit still's got the store tag on it!"

What a time they had that Saturday! Receipts for that one hour of shopping amounted to $450! However, the store had to close for the rest of the day to pick up and re-hang all that had been strewn about in the melee, plus make displays of the new inventory before reopening on Monday.

# ❦ Chapter 8

Luna was upset with herself. As she watched the excited customers leaving Tildy's with their bulging green bags, she gritted her teeth at a missed opportunity to create havoc and hysteria among the customers. She vowed to rectify her error the very next week.

She came into Tildy's on the following Wednesday around midday, a black slouch hat shading one side of her face. She carried a worn gray satchel purse and wore a shapeless gray dress and matronly lace-up shoes. She nodded curtly to Matilda and Jerlene, who were absorbed at the front desk, and then went over to the display of ladies' dresses. She fingered through them, glancing peripherally for any nearby customers. She then took a small box from her purse and shook it quickly on top of the rack of dresses before pressing the nozzle of a small spray bottle. She also opened a paper bag and put it between some dresses. Then, with her head down, she quickly exited out the front door. Matilda didn't pay her any special attention. Lots of people came in looking for a particular item and left.

Several customers were in the store as bow-tied, proper Mr. Ed Gregory pushed his obese diabetic wife, Penelope, around the store in a wheelchair. They went down the dress rack in search of a new muumuu or a queen-sized house dress when she let out a loud shriek. Something had skipped up onto one of her bare legs, and she began to stomp and slap at it while bouncing around in her wheelchair. Something had also traveled up the left pants leg of proper Mr. Gregory, which resulted in a slapping, shrieking, and hopping commotion that drew a small crowd. Matilda and Jerlene went over to see if a doctor was needed for a customer who was suffering a convulsion of some sort. At the same time, Miss Eva Nichols, who came in every week looking for donated crochet thread, threw the basket of accumulated thread balls into the air and started swatting at her breast saying "hopper grasses" and ants were in her underclothes. She was jumping up and down as crickets and colored balls of thread scrunched under her oxfords. People who didn't know what was happening started screaming and dashing for the door, resulting in a jam.

Mr. Gregory, bowtie askew, yelled out that he was going to sue Matilda for pain and suffering and also for the cost of a doctor's visit for Penelope, who was wheezing noisily as he wheeled her out the door.

Old Bertha Jones was nearby with a little basket of crocheted antimacassars she wanted to purchase. She had set the basket down on the floor to pull out a dress from the rack, and when she picked it up again, she saw ants crawling out of it. She pitched the basket and goods into the air and yelled, "I smell some rose perfume on these dresses!"

Bug-eyed customers screamed and dashed out the door jabbering noisily, "Ghosties! Ghosties!"

Chester, Magnolia, Vilma, and Annelise had hurried from the back when the melee started and were trying to make sense of what was going on, while Jerlene and Matilda were attempting to keep customers from trampling each other as they stampeded out.

#

Meanwhile, Luna stood across the street in the shadow of a large delivery truck parked beside Bi Rite Hardware. She watched with a wry smile thinking, *Now what are you going to do about that, Matilda!* She almost screamed out the name.

As she walked to her home on Mossy Point, near the river, she reviewed how easy it had been. A towheaded boy around ten years old had been standing in front of the Pup Tyme pet shop window looking at the playful terrier puppies cavorting there. She had been watching them also.

"Cute, aren't they?" she said to the boy.

"Yes, ma'am," he said. Then she asked his name, and he said "A.J."

"Do you like ice cream, A.J.?" She felt silly; all little boys liked ice cream.

His eyes lit up as he said, "Yes, ma'am."

She bent over to his approximate height and said, "I've got a pet lizard at home. Do you like lizards?"

"Yes, ma'am," he dimpled, looking at her.

"Well, if you will go into Pet Tyme and buy me three dollars' worth of crickets for my lizard, you can have the change and get yourself some ice cream from the Sweetie Pie Shop. Would you like that?" She gave him a five-dollar bill.

"Oh, yes, ma'am! Yes, ma'am! I'll go and get your crickets right now!"

He showed a broad toothy grin in delight at the chance to earn two dollars and get some ice cream. With that broad grin, he dashed into Pet Tyme and soon returned with the little cardboard container.

"Thank you, A.J. Enjoy your ice cream," she told him as he skipped happily toward the Sweetie Pie Shop.

She tapped the rustling box and said, "And now we'll get some little friends to join you."

When she got home, she got two slices of toasted bread, spread them with jelly, and put them near an ant hill in her backyard. It didn't take long for the ant-fest to begin. She then put on gloves and shoveled the encrusted bread and most of the anthill into a paper bag that she secured with a rubber band.

She smiled as she walked to Tildy's, pausing to look at the old-fashioned pink hollyhocks growing along the way. A pleasant little breeze brushed her cheek, but it was the rustling activity in the little box that made her smile. She had put the box into her large satchel purse and carried the paper bag in her hand.

Entering through the open front door, she passed Matilda and Jerlene, who were absorbed in organizing the supply of donated sacks used for bagging purchases. They didn't even notice her, so she went to the women's dresses section, pulled out a few of them, and placed some in front of her as if inspecting them for size and possible purchase. The bread slices and anthill sand had been quickly inserted between the dresses, and the box of crickets had been sprinkled into the entire rack as she moved the dresses back in pretense of looking for her size. It had all gone just exactly as she'd expected.

#

During the rest of the week, rumors were rampant that the ghost had shown up at Tildy's and had brought with it demonic bugs that attacked customers and left red bites on their legs and arms. It was reported that Mrs. Penelope Gregory had even been attacked in her wheelchair and had suffered a mild stroke. It was also said that her husband had sprained his ankle trying to rescue his wife and that the demonic bugs had invaded his clothing so that his pants were covered with a curious ectoplasmic substance that would not even burn in his fireplace, so he buried them. He told everybody who would listen that he was going to sue Matilda when his wife got better.

Children at school that week embellished what had occurred so that a devil with red horns had been seen lurking around the premises, and flames were coming from holes in the ground around the store. A greenish light was also said to be seen in the shop at midnight. Bertha Jones said she was sure the rose perfume was gaseous because she nearly suffocated when it brought on an asthma attack after she got home. Rumors abounded from the fanciful to the ridiculous.

The next day, Matilda hired Jimmy Wright of Be Gone Bugs! His pest extermination crew sprayed the rooms thoroughly. The dresses hanging on the affected rack had been hauled away to the town dump, and every corner and surface of the floors had been strongly disinfected with odorless bleach.

# Chapter 9

Matilda hoped this week would be uneventful after the trauma of the past week. The children walking past Tildy's en route to school were glancing over at the store curiously. A few children had stopped at the morning glory vine that grew on the fence near the store and were popping the buds between their thumbs and forefingers. Matilda remembered doing that when she was a child. Now she wondered how the flowers looked when they opened later. She'd never checked, but she thought it would be a pity if they were ragged and scraggly. *I never thought about that when I did it. Why did I do that? Was it just to hear the sound?*

She also remembered tying the legs of June bugs with string and swinging them against a big oak tree to batter them. Then she had set up "hospital beds" for them on leaves, and had gone into her mother's room to get perfume, lotion, and dusting powder to doctor them up. She held bug funerals when they died. *How cruel! Am I just a natural-born destroyer!? Is childhood innocence a myth? It should rightly be called childhood meanness.* Then she thought of the awful way she had bullied a girl and her friend in school, and she began to feel nauseous. She hadn't thought about them in a long time.

Jerlene was parking now, so Matilda shook off her troubling thoughts, unlocked the door, and went inside. Chester and the ladies had already come in through the donation room door. Matilda had called for a meeting thirty minutes before the store opened this morning. After greetings, coffee and donuts were shared, since Chester and the ladies had set up the fare in the used furniture room.

Matilda began, "I really hate to say this, but circumstances have led me to believe that there is someone set on malice who wants to close us down. People aren't comin' in like they used to. It's time we acknowledged that these things are being planned by somebody."

"Or some t'ing!" offered Vilma bug-eyed.

"Did you have the rooms blessed when you first moved in?" Jerlene asked.

"No," Matilda said. "I didn't even think of it."

"We need Reverend Sirrah from New Dawn to come in and bless it. It's never too late for a blessin'!" Jerlene said.

"And Pastor Grayson can do a exorcism too! He my pastor," said Magnolia.

"In de islands, we put out a glass of watah! De devil don' lak no watah! I keep de Bible open. Mus' be always open on a table beside yo' bed so no hants can come in." Vilma's eyes were wide in her face.

"But, Vilma, we know the devil can read. How's the Good Book going to keep him away? Didn't Satan use scripture when Jesus was in the wilderness? Oh, he's a lowdown, smart, and crafty ol' deceiver. That he is! But God is greater!" said Jerlene.

"Speak the Word of God! You know how Jesus used the Word when Satan came up against Him. If it was good enough for Jesus, it sure is good enough for us!" Annelise said.

As always, the ladies felt Annelise was right on the mark with her wise advice. It was then decided that Annelise would lead the group in prayer at the beginning of each staff meeting. Still, Matilda felt it was not a "what" but a "who" doing all of the mischief, and she vowed to get to the bottom of these malicious actions.

# 𝒮 Chapter 10

On the following Monday, the rich smell of a pipe bowl with burning cherry bark tobacco announced the arrival of a large, whiskered man in a dusty black derby hat with rheumy eyes set in skin like dried yellow parchment. He oozed into the room in a worn, rusty brown suit and old crinkled Florsheims that were run over at the heels and had slits cut out for the relief of his bunions. Jerlene wrinkled her nose and whispered to Matilda, whose lips were tightly pinched together, "What museum did he filch that old dusty derby from, I wonder!"

He was known as Miraculous Sam and stood in the doorway, smiling his huge horsey-like grin, showing off-white Chiclet teeth.

"I done come hyar to dribe dat ol' Satan out! To do a 'cism of dat evil debbil from da shop! Where he done ack up at?" A customer pointed toward the area of the dresses.

He then proceeded to fan the crowd back, away from the area where the last smell of roses had been detected. The crowd moved in a wave and gawked as he took on an unworldly and trembly tone of voice, calling out, "O debbil! O debbil! Git yo' ugly evil self outa heah!"

He surveyed the area with jerky head movements. Then he took out a little gray pouch and sprinkled some powder from it with his ham-like right hand, making a large circle. Next he took some pig bones out of another pouch he carried. He threw the bones into the air above the circle. The customers moved far back with their mouths agape, and some of the women clutched or hid behind each other.

"Y'all get back now! Get on back! He goan run thoo 'at back doah yonda!" he pointed. Then conspiratorially, he half whispered, "Y'all watch 'im now! Watch 'im!"

As the customers gawked with wide eyes toward the door, old Sam took his foot and kicked up the powder. "See 'im? See? Dere he go! Dere he go! He lef' he smoke. Doan smell it, y'all, 'cause you can get possess!"

The customers were speechless and didn't move. Then Old Sam ambled over to the cashier's desk, held his dusty ham-like hand out, and said, "Miz Tildy, ah chahges ten dollahs fuh my 'cisms."

Matilda looked at him sternly and said, "I didn't hire you to come in here to do any exorcism! Now you just git, and don't you ever come back in here scaring my customers, you hear?" She was red-faced, and her voice was loud with authority.

Several pairs of eyes followed him as he shuffled out muttering something about some people having "no 'preciation a'tall," and saying loudly as he exited, "Don't y'all come lookin' fuh me to help y'all when death comes a-creepin' in yo' room!"

"Jerlene, go get Chester from the back room and have him come out here and clean up this mess!"

As Chester swept the area and then used a damp dust mop, he moved the rack aside and saw big dead water bugs dropping onto the floor from the clothing hanging there.

The mortified customers standing by drew back in disgust, exclaiming words of vexation as they saw what was accumulating. Looking at her with accusing eyes, somebody said sharply, "Tildy, what's all this? Didn't you say you got this place exterminated?"

"Maybe they dropped off of ol' Sam!" someone called out sardonically.

"Jerlene, go get the ladies from the back!" Matilda said, tightening her lips.

Magnolia, Velma, and Annelise came into the room wonderingly. They had been standing in the doorway stupefied when Miraculous Sam was doing his farcical activity.

"What on earth?" "Well, I never!" " How that mess get on da flo'?" they all said in concert.

"Did you all see any bugs in the clothes back there?" Matilda asked.

"No, *ma'am*! Every now and then, we find a dead water bug from a box somebody had in their garage, but nothing else!" Annelise said.

"We wouldn't put nothin' on no hangers less'n it be in good shape and clean!" Magnolia said emphatically.

"Ebry grin teet' don mean laff, my mudder say in geechie. Somebody done come here for mess up," Velma offered.

"I believe you're right, Velma. I know you ladies are good about checking things out, but somebody is up to no good. Keep your eyes out for anything suspicious or for anybody lurking about and acting strange. You too, Jerlene and Chester. I'm sure gonna prosecute if we find out who keeps doing these things!"

They racked their brains and made lists as they recalled strange-acting customers or those who had become irate over something about a purchase or a transaction. They compared their lists and did not come up with anyone who they felt was malicious or angry enough to have done these things. Becoming even more vigilant, they watched every possible suspicious move, and mirrors were installed in various locations so that areas might be scanned more scrupulously.

One day in the late afternoon, Vilma said, "I been t'inkin." Her eyes were wide and darted back and forth. "I t'ink it be the lady with da scarf on her face. She mebbe do the hoodoo. I t'ink she do it wit' de evil eye behind 'at scarf. She be here early too! If folkses get de hair and de nail parings, and a pitcher of you, you be done for. It be a pow'rful evil." Annelise told Vilma that the woman with the scarfed face ventured into Tildy's at times of the day before people got off from work to avoid stares and whispers.

"She told me that she didn't want any pity. She believed that people thought her husband beat her since her face was partially covered, but it was because her mouth and chin were so badly scarred from a grease fire in her kitchen."

Annelise, full of compassion, had seen her at Bi Rite Grocery and went out of her way to engage her in conversation. The woman had opened up to her, sensing her kind spirit. Now Annelise said, "It's not her. I know her. She has a sad story, but she's not a vindictive woman."

# ⚛ Chapter 11

Saturday mornings always brought in school-age children who wanted to see what new toys and gadgets had been donated. This morning, two little boys came in swinging June bugs on strings. They were buzzing noisily, and as the boys made convolutions with their bugs, one hit little Pete in the forehead. He was sure he had been mortally wounded and fell down in a tantrum as his mother and Matilda came to the scene.

Their father, Big Hank, came over to the area.

"What's goin' on over here?" His big beefy face held bleary eyes.

Matilda said, "These boys have to take those June bugs outside. It's causin' too much commotion."

"Wal, the boys just wanna have a little fun. You 'member how it used to be, doncha?"

Magnolia had stuck her head out toward the area, and she said to Annelise, "Somebody ought to go outside and get a branch off that willer tree 'cross the street and tear them boys up. They don't mind nobody!"

Chester was also at the door, and he called out, "Hey, Hank! Let's go outside a minute. Come on, boys!"

They went outside with Chester just as the chubby twins, Horace and Horatio, were coming in with their parents. On the way out the door, they stuck their tongues out and made faces at the twins, who looked at them curiously and walked on with their parents. They were smart little boys and always went to the children's book section or to the comics section where they would sometimes find classics. Their parents were substitute teachers who rented a guest house on the property of a white family living on Oak Heights. When there was no substitute work, they were paid for working as handyman and maid for the white family.

It amused Matilda when she recalled how the boys had once set up an imaginary schoolroom in front of Tildy's. Both aspired to be schoolteachers, and on that day of pretending, Horace sat on a wooden crate, acting as principal. Horatio sat behind a lengthwise crate, acting as teacher. A few curious children had gathered as "students" while the teacher lectured and then questioned them on why trees took off all of their clothing in winter and put them on in the hot summer.

Jim Higgins fidgeted with the loose middle button of his soiled, green plaid flannel shirt and cleared his throat to announce himself as if coming through the door for a top management interview at Tildy's. Customers had been rather sparse since the so-called demon incident, but Jim told everybody that he wasn't afraid of "no bugs." People called him Boss Higgins because he always carried a large, battered attaché case. He wore no cap on his thick rusty hair, which was nappy like his grizzled beard. His wide face exposed yellow pegs that passed for teeth alongside gaps on his top and bottom gums. His stomach rolled over his broken belt, which hitched up his pants. His small, stringy-haired and cowed wife, dressed in faded calico, followed behind him with a sad and sallow face. Two thin and hollow-cheeked barefoot boys trailed behind her.

"Mornin'," he greeted Jerlene and Matilda at the cashier's desk. "Need a new business suit today. Got a big meetin' goin' on tomorrow—quarterly conference. What y'all got?"

"Got some nice nearly new gabardine ones over there on the corner rack." Jerlene pointed to the polyester, corduroy, seersucker, old wool, and gabardine assortment. "Go through them. Might find your size."

He started to walk over on old rundown loafers that had been slit near the little toes because the shoes were too narrow.

"We got some nice boys' sandals in today too," Matilda said. "Might fit your boys."

"Hit's after the first of June," he snarled. "Boys don't need no shoes." Matilda understood what he meant. Many children looked forward to the first day of June when they began to go barefoot for the summer, freeing their little cramped toes until it was time for school in September again. The local parents all seemed to agree on this as the magic date. Many of the parents complained that their children outgrew their shoes fast and that the children were also hard on them, scuffing them and such. They were glad they had a respite from buying so often. The boys usually were the hardest on their brogans and wore them with flapping soles or open fronts with the toes out if there was no money for new ones. Some put cardboard in the bottoms to cover the holes and hoped it wouldn't rain. If the school shoes were outgrown, they would be passed down to one of the younger siblings, even if a little paper had to be stuffed in the toes. Then their feet would graduate to their Sunday schools—if they had any and if they still fit. Most of the children only had one pair, however.

"You done got enough! Don't ye ask fer no more!" Jim snarled at his family as they stood at the checkout counter with their meager goods. "Enough I say!"

The big bewhiskered man's wife seemed to slink down as she held two ten-cent dog-eared romance paperback books for purchase. The two thin boys behind her had a plastic truck and a toy fire engine.

He haggled with Jerlene about the prices of the toys. The plastic truck had paint chipped off the sides, and the fire engine had a wobbly wheel that was about to jiggle off. Instead of paying twenty-five cents apiece, he finally paid a dime for each, Jerlene having tired of haggling for so minor a sale. He rifled through the pages of the paperback books his wife had selected and pronounced them in good condition. He had selected for himself a dust-colored polyester suit and a chartreuse green tie. His purchases totaled $5.40. He proudly told his family that he'd treat them to popsicles since he'd gotten such good buys today. He emptied his pocket of some change, a dried dead roach, and some string. Then he selected three dimes and two nickels, putting them down on the counter. He picked up the bag containing his suit and necktie and began to shuffle toward the front door.

"Wait!" Jerlene yelled after him, "You didn't pay for your suit and tie!"

His grizzled beetle brows clumped up like dried moss, and his voice boomed out, "Yes, I did! I give you a bill and also some change for the other! Don't you try to cheat me or call me a liar!" His look was menacing, and a spray of garlicky spittle shot from his mouth. His scrawny wife and scared boys scrunched down a bit as if to fend off a wayward blow or two, and some of the startled customers looked on furtively.

"I'm not trying to cheat you or call you a name, but I think maybe you just forgot," Jerlene answered him mildly.

"I didn't fergit. I ne'er fergit!" he raged from his bluish-red face. "You cheaters! You gonna rue this day. You just wait and see!"

He stomped his way out the door, followed fearfully by his family who toddled behind and stole glances back at Jerlene with blanched faces and wide eyes.

Matilda heard the commotion as she came from the lavatory. She arched her brows and asked, "Now what was that all about?"

Jerlene recounted the scene, sighed, and then said, "Well, I guess we lost five dollars and gained an enemy."

Matilda shook her head and clucked her tongue. "We sure do get all kinds, don't we, Jer?"

"And this one made a threat and just happened to have a dead roach on him. Bears some watchin' if he ever comes back in here!"

# ❦ Chapter 12

On a beautiful Sunday afternoon, Luna decided to take a walk and found herself in the Beantown section, admiring a beautiful rose garden that was in front of the green and white clapboard Flora Rose Boarding House. An older black woman with a peach-colored face and hair dyed the color of cinnamon came out onto the porch, her cane steadying her.

"Well, hello, child! How you this fine mornin'?"

"Oh, just fine, ma'am. These are the most beautiful roses!"

"Yes, they're my pride and joy. I'm Ola Mae Fields, and this is my home. My dear deceased husband gave me my first rosebush years ago, and I've been planting more each time a new color comes out. See this beauty?" She pointed to a large yellow bloom with pink edges. "It's called the Peace Rose. And over here is Joseph's Coat." she pointed to a bush with three different colors on each bloom. "Now, my favorite is this one," she said delightedly, pointing to a deep purple one. "It's called the Black Rose. Oh, I could go on and on about my roses, child." She laughed heartily, flashing a gold tooth.

"Here. Let's cut you a bouquet to take home."

Then she handed Luna the pruning shears saying, "Matter of fact, you can cut your own while I go inside and get some paper for you to carry them home in. Oh, what did you say your name was?"

"I'm Luna Carter, Mrs. Fields"

"Call me Ola Mae."

"Yes, ma'am."

The deep purple of the Black Rose was luxuriant, and its petals felt like velvet. It made Luna think of Cora Jane, the only person who was kind to her during their elementary school years. She had moved to Hortonville and came into the fourth-grade class late in the year.

Cora Jane was very dark. In fact, Luna had never seen a colored girl so dark. Cora Jane was taunted too. Some of the girls looked at her and said, "Ooga Booga!" Then they did weird little dances like they'd seen in a Tarzan serial. The boys would hide behind the corner of the school building and yell out "Sambo!" One little colored boy who was not very dark told her she must have come out of one of the coke ovens.

Luna saw her hanging her head and crying at times. When Cora told Mrs. Sirrah the children were picking on her, Mrs. Sirrah told her to just ignore them, that they were just ignorant, but that didn't stop them, and Luna could tell that it hurt her just the same. One time, Luna heard Cora Jane say to them, "The blacker the berry, the sweeter the juice." That stopped them for a day or so. Mrs. Sirrah had seated her in the back opposite Luna. She had placed Luna there so that when she raised her hand to ask or answer a question, no one would notice her hand much and start smirking and whispering.

Cora Jane had asked her about her hands, if the fingers grew there after she was born and if they hurt. She had told her they didn't hurt and that she'd always had them. She let Cora Jane feel them. She wasn't afraid to touch them and said that she didn't care about them. "We can still be friends," she had said.

Recess often found them sitting on the grassy part of the playground, sharing confidences. They never joined the games because the other girls would not pick them for ring games where hands had to be held—like Red Rover, Here Comes the King a-Riding, or Little Sally Walker.

One Monday at recess, Cora Jane taught a song to Luna. She had learned it in her Sunday School class. It was:

*Jesus loves the little children,*
*All the children of the world.*
*Red and yellow, black and white,*
*They are precious in His sight.*
*Jesus loves the little children*
*Of the world.*

Her voice was so beautiful and pure that it stopped the conversation of a group of girls nearby. They seemed fascinated by her lovely voice, and some began to sing it with her. They had learned it in their Sunday school classes too. Luna did not attend a Sunday school, so she asked her mother if she could go with Cora Jane. There she had learned so many new things, but the most wonderful thing of all was learning that God loved her just as she was.

At school, it was the pretty girl with the fat blonde curls and dimples who was the meanest of all. She was stuck up and acted like she was better than everybody else. Her name was Matilda. She spread the rumor that Luna had touched a baby, and now it had grown extra toes. She said that her mother had actually seen the baby. She also spread the rumor that Luna could work black magic from her small fingers, and that sparks flew out from them when she was around a black cat.

Little groups were always clustered around Matilda as she reported things she said people had seen or knew about Looney Luna and Crazy Cora. One time she said, "Cora Jane's been teaching her something called mojo magic. I saw a little hoodoo doll sticking out of her pocket. Don't ever let her have a strand of your hair because she can put it into a bucket of chicken blood under a full moon in the graveyard, and then you will be under her spell!"

The little gaggle of girls all said, "Ooh!" and shuddered as they whispered about it. Creative imaginations embellished the information. Luna found out about some of this from a note that had been passed and dropped. The girls distanced themselves from Cora Jane and Luna at recess and lunchtime and asked their teacher to let them move their seats closer to the front.

# Chapter 13

It had hurt Geneva Carter to see Luna coming home in tears so often, so she came up with the idea of having her wear cut-off gloves. She bought several pairs of short white gloves so that Luna would always have a clean pair. The tiny fingers would be hidden under the gloves above the bottom joint of her little fingers. The gloves would also be cut off at the bottom of the second finger joint for the rest of both hands. Geneva embroidered them and stitched tiny ruffled trim around the wrists. While stitching, she told Luna that it was all right to be different, that some birthmarks were inside and some were outside. She pointed to her left ear and showed Luna that it had no lobe. Luna had never noticed that before. Geneva said that her own mother told her that she had seen a snake when she was pregnant with her, and she had touched her ear in fright; hence, the birthmark occurred, or so it had been related. She felt, however, that this was an old wives' tale.

When the Carters came to school to talk with the teacher, Mrs. Sirrah said she did all she could to keep the children from name calling and bullying by keeping some inside during recess, making them stay after school, having them write essays about respect, and calling parents. Still, the children found ways to be hurtful. She said that she and a fellow teacher had been discussing hurtful teasing and bullying, and they decided to introduce a plan they were going to implement. They would share their plan at the next district teachers' seminar to be held in two weeks.

There was an ugly scene in Luna and Cora's social studies class after Mr. Diggs said, "In America, anybody can grow up to be president if they were born here."

Ricky, a wisecracker, asked sarcastically, "Even a woman?" Then his friend Ryan said, "Anybody but a nigger!" Some of the students tittered, but Luna thought wryly, *And never a woman with twelve fingers!*

Mr. Diggs had Ryan stay after school and write "I will respect others" on the chalkboard one hundred times.

Their common misery brought the two girls together as the very best of friends. They decided to wear the same colors to school and made clothes calendars together: red for Monday, then blue, yellow, green, and finally multicolor for Friday. They had seen the movie *Pinky* and decided to walk gracefully like Jeanne Crain did—left step, then a left hip bone thrust; right step, then a right hip bone thrust. They practiced while walking across the Horton River Bridge, oblivious of the stares of motorists driving by. After a while, that became tiresome, so they decided to practice walking by swinging the left arm forward with the left leg, and vice versa. The stiff movements brought roars from Ryan and his friends who had piled into an old jalopy driving across the bridge. They yelled out "Inky Pinky Robots!" and guffawed.

When the girls got close to Cora Jane's house, Luna noticed that Cora had become very quiet, and her eyes looked moist as she went over to sit in the porch swing. Luna sat beside her, and when she inquired, Cora began to cry and said, "Doesn't anybody care about my feelings? Am I just worthless? Why did God make me so dark? Will people always look at me and hate me instead of knowing who I really am? I don't want to be a president anyway! Maybe I'll just be a famous singer, and if I don't have me a bathroom, then I'll have to hire Ryan to clean out my diamond-covered slop jar!"

She and Luna began to laugh and laugh until their stomachs hurt.

# ৸ Chapter 14

Luna recalled a subsequent week when things changed and she actually began to smile. Mrs. Sirrah announced a special program that was going to begin immediately in her classroom. She called it The Pledge and explained that the principal liked her idea and that other teachers were considering using it in their classrooms as well.

Luna and Cora listened as she began to discuss the procedure. They hoped it would not make things worse for them. Mrs. Sirrah assigned each student to a small group in a semi-circle. She then appointed one student to sit in the middle for five minutes. Luna hoped it wouldn't be her or Cora, but strangely to her, the students Mrs. Sirrah picked to sit in the middle of the circles were the worst offenders in the class, who now proudly felt like they were special. They were told to pull out a slip of paper from a box. Unknown to them beforehand, conditions/handicaps were printed on the slip. The slip was read aloud, and the other students in the semicircle were directed to taunt/tease him about the condition written on the slip. He was told to be silent until five minutes had elapsed. Mrs. Sirrah would ring a bell at the end of the time allotted.

When the taunting began, some who sat in the middle of the circle became red-faced in anger, and others teared up. Mrs. Sirrah then had all of those in the circle sit in a line up front and tell how they felt when they were the recipients of the teasing.

"I was mad! That wasn't right!"

"I wanted to fight."

"It hurt me."

The reports varied. Then Mrs. Sirrah asked, "Do we all agree that words can hurt?"

The class responded as one, "Yes, Mrs. Sirrah."

"What can we do to make sure no one is hurt by our words? Do you have any suggestions?"

Cora and Luna had sat silently but open-mouthed in two different groups.

Mrs. Sirrah stood at the board, chalk in hand, to write suggestions such as "Make 'em stay in," "Make 'em write," "Call their mother," and "Tell on 'em."

"Wonderful! Ryan, you had your hand up."

Proud of being called on first, Ryan stood up and said, "We will not call people names."

Then others came up with statements that Mrs. Sirrah wrote on the board. Luna was proud that her classmates really knew how to be kind. She looked over at Cora, who was actually smiling.

"We have quite a few great ideas! Thank you! Now, I will give each of you a laminated copy of our class pledge tomorrow, and I will post one in our room. Suppose someone doesn't honor it? Suppose someone forgets?"

"Make 'em stay after school."

"We can tell them not to do it!"

"Hit 'em in the mouth!"

"No, we won't do that, Betty."

"Tell you what. If we go two weeks with no teasing or bullying, I will ask the principal if I can treat the class to a pizza party. Okay?"

"Oh boy!" "Yes!" "That's what I'm talkin' 'bout!" the class exclaimed. They were ecstatic and pledged to make it work!

Luna and Cora felt good. The pledge was honored and made a difference, but Luna's mother still parked the old Ford near the school to drive her and Cora home if necessary.

The wonderful pizza party was held after school. Parents had heard about the pledge party and had come to assist after school, bringing lemonade and punch. Mrs. Sirrah's plan caught on, and some other teachers decided to use it too.

A month after this exercise, Mrs. Sirrah also implemented a "You're the Star" program with the principal's blessing. The class looked forward to it, but individual students were nervous. Luna and Cora were especially so.

Once a week, a student was called to come up to the front. A plastic crown would be placed on his/her head, and each student in the class would have to say something nice about him/her. No one could duplicate what somebody else said. Luna and Cora were scared that they'd be called to come up front and asked to go to the restroom every time the exercise began, but no one was permitted to go until after the exercise.

The day came when Luna was the star, and she went up front timidly, looking down at her feet. The crown was set on her head, and the class was totally silent as the first person began to speak.

"She has on a real pretty dress."

"I like the way she wears her hair."

"She's kind."

"She's quiet."

"She makes good grades."

After a while, they were trying hard to find positive things that were not duplicates, but they managed. She was relieved when she left the front, happy no one was mean.

When Cora came up, the first thing that was said referred to her beautiful voice, and Cora even ventured a little smile at that. Both Cora and Luna loved that year in Mrs. Sirrah's classroom. Their happiness was broken only by the remembrance that, although Matilda wasn't a part of that classroom, she was still a horror outside on the playground.

# ✑ Chapter 15

Sales were always up around the holidays, and Halloween was coming up at the end of the next week. Pumpkins appeared in front of some homes ready for the carving of their Halloween grins and grimaces. Costumes were big sale items, and most of the ones at Tildy's had been sold out already, since those at retail establishments had nearly doubled in price. With so many people out of work in Hortonville, Tildy's was the place to shop.

Fall festivals at the churches and schools had been replacing neighborhood trick-or-treating on Halloween, since razor blades and needles had been found in some of the apples in recent years. Even bobbing for apples had been curtailed now because of the possibility of catching the flu or a cold from the saliva of the participants dunking in the big tub.

Matilda said to her staff, "Y'all know that Halloween is the witches' Sabbath, don't you? We have to make sure no real mischief is done to Tildy's, masquerading as some haunting. It would be good if we could hire some security people to supervise the building that night."

"Do you think we'll be okay for Soap Night?" Jerlene asked.

"Well, we can always get the soap off, and some of these buildings could stand a good hosing down anyway," Matilda said as she chuckled. "Soap Night has never been a problem so far as I know."

She still remembered going out on Soap Night herself. It was the night before Halloween, when the young people would go into the downtown section and write messages on the shop windows with pieces of soap. The messages were usually about who was in love with whom or just their initials written in hearts. It had never been anything but "clean" fun along with hayrides and marshmallow and weenie roasts.

Matilda decided to close the store on Wednesday and purchased security lights, which were mounted around the premises to deter anyone who might be up to malice for Halloween on Friday. Chester volunteered to sit in his truck and watch the shop on Halloween night. Magnolia said, "I'll see if my husband, Roy, would be willing to act as some kinda security too. He need to have somethin' to do."

Matilda's eyes were bright as she said, "You know, that gives me an idea! Do you think Roy would be willing to work here as a security person with all the stuff that's been happenin'? I could get him a uniform and provide his lunch and a small salary if he'd be willing."

"Why, that's a wonderful idea, Tildy! I'll ask him this evenin'. He's okay 'cept for the silicosis in his lungs from the coal dust in the mines, and that's not catchin'. It does give him coughin' spells sometimes. Could he sit in the front room if he gets a little winded?"

"He sure could, 'Nolia. We got at least one comfortable chair in the furniture room that we could put out front here for him."

Roy had enthusiastically agreed, so the next day he went with Tildy to the surplus store to be outfitted. He even had a badge inscribed "Security" and a walkie-talkie with reception available in the back room and also at the main desk. Attired for work in his blue uniform and silver badge, his well-groomed gray hair and trim gray moustache made him look every bit the consummate official security personnel, and the ladies felt even safer with two men on the premises now. With Roy and Chester on patrol for Halloween, the holiday passed uneventfully.

The week afterwards, the two men hauled boxes stored with Christmas decorations down from the rafters, and Jerlene and Tildy boxed up the few remaining Halloween items that were unsold. The ladies in the back packed up incoming plastic jack-o-lanterns and costumes now being donated for next year.

Matilda said to Jerlene, "So many people forget to be thankful at Thanksgiving in the rush to get to gift-giving and gift-getting for Christmas. We don't have much to display for Thanksgiving, Jerlene."

"I have a straw cornucopia and a plaster Indian man and woman at home that I can bring and put out for display, but not for sale," Jerlene said.

"And I can bring some artificial fruit and veggies for the cornucopia from home too, or I'll just buy some. I've got a plastic turkey and a Pilgrim couple at home somewhere. I'll look for them and bring them in too," Matilda added.

They hustled to get the Christmas items out, knowing that these would be purchased quickly, since new department store decorations were too costly for the many people who were out of work. Customers began coming in the week after Halloween to get ready for the next festive season, since the two upcoming holidays were only a month apart.

#

No one was at the counter today when Luna entered Tildy's. Jerlene and Tildy were busy hanging red, green, and silver garlands in the store. She went to the desk and put her purse and a little bag down on it as she pretended to admire the Thanksgiving panoply of an overflowing cornucopia and the Native American couple and Pilgrims. She was startled when Roy came up behind her.

"Oh! You startled me!" she said. Then she smiled and added, "This is such a nice display for Thanksgiving."

"Yes," Roy said. "It will be here before you know it. It's just around the corner."

She then picked up her purse and the bag and walked over to the infants' and toddlers' clothing bins. She held up some little shirts, sleepers, and bibs as if examining them for purchase. Then she put the small bag in the bottom of the bin surreptitiously and opened it. Peripherally, she saw some young women advancing toward the area, so she left hastily, going over to the linens and domestics area. Soon, she heard screams and shrieks coming from the infants' clothing area. Two women were shaking the clothing and throwing them on the floor. Live and dying fishing worms, some Gummi worms, and dried rose petals were mixed in the bins with the clothing, and some of the young women thought they were seeing baby snakes. Jerlene and Tildy rushed over to the melee and into the scent of roses again.

"Oh, no! Not again!" they exclaimed.

Chester and Roy came in to deal with this latest episode, and the ladies in the back came out wide-eyed, shaking their heads.

Matilda asked if anyone had noted suspicious or strange-acting persons in the store. No one had, but all of a sudden, Roy said, "You know, there was a real nice lady who was admiring the display on the counter, and come to think of it, a worm was wiggling near the cornucopia when I passed the counter later."

Jerlene and Matilda looked at him with widened eyes and nervously questioned him. He said he'd never seen the lady before and that she appeared to be very nice. He described her and said he was sure he would recognize her if he saw her again.

He said, "These things mos'ly seem to happen 'roun' ladies' things, 'cept the babies bins. I b'lieve we should start jus' lookin' at the women folks."

Matilda and Jerlene mused and then said, "You've got a point there, Roy. That's the best observation yet!"

# ◊ Chapter 16

The town was full of goose bumps today instead of festivity as the holiday season neared. Bertha Jones, who had last been in Tildy's during the ants/crickets incident and had vowed that she'd never come back, rushed into the shop screaming, "My grandchildren! Have you s-seen my t-two grandchildren??" Trista and Babs, eight and ten years of age, had been visiting Bertha for a few weeks. Now they were missing!

Bertha's face was swollen from crying. She was kneading her faded apron and still had rollers in her hair. All of the customers gave her their undivided attention.

"When did you last see them, Bertha, and what were they wearing?" Matilda asked.

"A-after supper last night, they said they were going to take a walk down to the corner and c-come right back. I- I told them okay and n-not to g-get in nobody's car. Then I fell asleep in m-my rock-rocker, and when I got up to go to b-bed, I just assumed they were a-asleep upstairs.

"Th-they h-had bl-blue j-jeans on an' an' yell-yellow T-shirts. Did anybody s-see them?" A freshet of tears gave way.

The customers were clearly concerned. No one remembered seeing them. Jerlene called the police department and was told that somebody would be at Tildy's right away and to try to calm Mrs. Jones and the customers.

En route to Tildy's, Police Chief Martin and Deputy Myers heard on their car radios that Dirk Willer, a prisoner who was part of a road work crew, had escaped. He was a convicted human trafficker.

When the officers got to Tildy's, Doctor Martin had been called to attend Bertha, who was having an asthmatic attack, certain that her grandchildren had been kidnapped by the escapee.

Willer's description was disseminated, and pictures of him were posted immediately on the telephone poles, in the bank, and in the post office. He was a hard-faced twenty-four-year-old man with staring eyes. A $5,000 reward was posted for information leading to his capture. An additional $5,000 was posted for information regarding the whereabouts of the two missing girls whose school pictures appeared on other posters.

No one slept easy in Hortonville. Each little creak outside a house raised a start from the people who lived inside. At Tildy's, Chester said the police ought to check out Violet's house because she'd let anybody in who had breath and britches. That brought about a round of tittering laughter.

Rumors were rampart. Somebody said that he had holed up in New Dawn Church in Beantown. A teenage boy said he was sure that a person matching Willer's description had been seen going in and out of the privy behind Mrs. Pauline's Music Conservatory. (That was where Mrs. Pauline's first husband had been bitten by a snake and died. Nobody in the town went in there anymore.)

It was Chester, however, who discovered Willer's hideout, which led to his capture and to the recovery of the two girls he had with him. Chester always liked trains, and one day at lunch he went to sit on a grassy mound near the railroad tracks to watch the N&W cars go by. The tracks were parallel to the coke ovens, which were not burning on this particular day. A high girlish laugh was heard from one of the ovens, and in the space between two coupled cars, he saw a doughy white face and arm reach out and pull someone back. He scrambled up from the grassy mound and hurried to the nearest telephone booth where he dialed 911 and gave the information to the police department.

Officers sped to the area and arrested Willer speedily. The girls were unhurt. Willer had shown them some pictures of Shirley Temple from his wallet, and they had been told that he had contacts in Hollywood and promised to put them in movies like Shirley Temple. They were at the railroad tracks to hop an open car for a ride to California, they'd been told.

A collective sigh and tears of relief came from families in all parts of the county, and now Chester was a hero. He received the reward as well as the recovery funds and was now the talk of Tildy's. Customers beamed at him as if he were royalty, and people came to the workroom to shake his hand. He even let the Harmonettes kiss him on the cheek.

For a week, whenever he heard Violet's syrupy voice from one of the outer rooms, he excused himself to go to the lavatory. She decided to fix up a basket for him and leave it on the counter. The accompanying envelope was addressed: "To Chester, a real man! My hero!" Inside was a flowery card signed with her name and a lipsticked kiss, as well as little sample packs of men's colognes that she had collected from department stores in Johnson City.

Violet, powdered and rouged, wanted to make sure Chester had received her basket, so she loitered in Tildy's on the pretext of looking at the new items that had arrived. She heard a woman talking to another one under her breath, "That old hag. I can see what she finds in Chester. He's the greatest looking guy ever, but she's so pitiful, making big cow eyes and simpering around him!"

Violet heard the comment, made a mouth, and tossed her head so that one hairpiece came half loose and threatened to slide down her temple. She then proceeded to the donation room, holding a blouse on the pretext of asking about its price, since there was no tag on it.

She ignored the "Can we help you?" that came from Annelise. Instead, she sashayed over to the table where Chester was trying out some donated lamps. She touched him on the arm and said in a saccharine voice, "Oh, Chester, you're so smart and so brave too! Did you get my basket?"

He looked up and said, "Oh, hello, Vi'let. Yes I did. Thank you so much. How you been doing?"

"Fine," she trilled. "You busy tonight, hon?" One of her false lashes had loosened and looked like a wriggling spider above her left eye as she fluttered it.

Magnolia spoke up loudly and sternly, "Employees only in here. Didn't you see the new sign outside the door? We don't want nobody tripping over the 'quipment and donations all crowded up in here!"

Violet puffed loudly and rolled her eyes. "And just who are you—the back alley manager now?"

Magnolia swelled up at this, and her eyes threatened to pop out of her head.

"Lady, you better git outa my face, an' I mean git now!"

She was coming from behind the table when Annelise touched her on the arm and said softly, "'Nolia, girl, she just sad, just sad. Let it go. Let it go."

Somehow the tone of Annelise's voice diffused Magnolia's anger and she stopped midway, glaring at the back of the retreating Violet and mumbling, "That hussy just trying to get some of that reward money Chester got! That's all!"

Chester had not mentioned his plans for the reward money. The employees in Tildy's wondered, but they all respected his privacy.

Vilma had hauled over from the floor a bulging bag from the pile of donations. As she pulled out some dirty items, she wrinkled her nose and said, "Where people shame? Dey t'row out da donations and give us dey trash! Somebuddy musta done died! Deseyuh smell lak a cawspse in da bag!"

While dragging the bag closer to the door for Chester to put it in the dumpster, the screeching of rusty wheels got her attention and revealed a covered pushcart driven by the ponderous bulk of Miraculous Sam.

"Well, what for you come, Mister Miracle?" Vilma asked.

"We sho' don't need yo' 'cisms again!" Magnolia yelled out. "So you jus' take yo' tricks and fly on outa heah!"

Miraculous had parked his cart and was now at the open door saying, "Now, now, now jus' hol' on, Miz Nolie. I done started up my new café, and I got some samples fuh you to taste."

Annelise stopped pulling curtains from a box and put her hands on her hips. "You goin' freegan again?" He knew she meant collecting "free meat" from highway roadkill.

He ignored the question and retrieved from his cart a tray of barbecued meat that smelled very appetizing.

"Smells good. What restaurant dumpster you been divin' in?" asked Magnolia.

"Ain't been in no dumpster. The good Lord done provide me a better source. It's true I get some of ma fruit that be a little bruised from behind Valu Market, but ma meat's provided by da Lord, and it be real fresh. Want a piece o' rack of rabbit? It's fresh barbecued. How 'bout some possum meat wit' da sweet pertaters side it to sweeten up da meat? I gots 'em right here in ma cart."

Vilma spoke up quickly, "I knows it. I jus' knows it for true! You be freegan! I see da hair done riz up on yo' neck. Now don't get de long mout' cause I done foun' you out. Tell de trut'!" She pointed a long finger directly at him.

He moved closer into the room, cocked his head to the side, then said, "Don't y'all think it's wrong to ignore da goodness da Lord puts out fuh ya? Now this heah is fresh meats. Fresh killed right side da highway. Hit ain't no old tainty meat an' not stiff neither. Da possum was right up da road 'bout a mile. Da blood was still warm. I cooks 'em on high flame to kill any juhms. Let me heist you up a piece outa ma cart an' show you what I got so you can tek a taste."

He put a hand in the cart and pulled out a roasted piece of what looked like an animal's leg.

Annelise looked at it with horror and said, "How do you know that animal wasn't sick? It could have had rabies or something!"

Vilma said, "If you come 'roun' up heah wit' da foamin' at da mouf, we all goan know for sho'!"

Magnolia added, "Next thing we know you'll be in here with cheese and grub worms callin' it some macaroni! Now git on outa heah!" She held up the steam attachment and aimed it in his direction.

Old Sam scurried to get out of the way. He was holding the piece of roast high in the air and nearly did a wheelie scrambling to get out of the line of Magnolia's aim. He yelled back at her saying, "You crazy, lady! You crazy!"

When he had gone, sixty-year-old Magnolia began to fan herself furiously, saying, "I do declare he done brought back my hot flashes on me!"

Matilda, Jerlene, and even Chester and Roy nearly doubled over in laughter when the ladies told them about Miraculous Sam's Traveling Roadkill Restaurant.

# ❦ Chapter 17

The song her mother used to sing came back to her so often these days that Luna wondered if her mother was singing to comfort her from heaven. She walked to the bank of the Horton River, took a small twig, and began stirring in the shallows as she softly sang it too.

*In the gloaming, O, my darling,*
*When the lights are dim and low,*
*And the quiet shadows falling,*
*Softly come and softly go.*
*When the winds are sobbing faintly*
*With a gentle, unknown woe,*
*Will you think of me and love me*
*As you did once long ago?*

Vilma was hunting long grass to make some baskets as the mothers had taught all of their daughters on John's Island and as she had done when her husband had the basketry business. She spied a young woman with a dipper that she was using to pour water from the shallows into a mason jar. The woman turned her head around toward the sound of the rustling grass, but apparently she did not see anyone. Vilma, however, did see her, but she did not recognize her as someone she knew.

#

Two days later in the early afternoon, Johnny Mack minced into Tildy's, clad in a powder blue polyester suit, a Hawaiian shirt, and a peach-colored tie. He tossed his long, curly bleached hair behind his right ear, said, "Hello, girls!" to Matilda and Jerlene at the front desk, and proceeded directly to the ladies' shoes.

Jerlene followed en route to inspect the girls' clothing racks nearby for empty hangers, when over his shoulder, Johnny trilled, "Any high fashion heels come in for my sister, dear?"

"Not unless you want to look at those patent leather platforms," she said, pointing to them. "I think they came in recently."

She lifted her eyebrows slightly. She knew Johnny had no sister.

"They don't look like a 9½, my dear. You know my sister wears 9½."

"I think they're bigger than they look, Johnny."

When Jerlene went back to collecting empty hangers, Johnny furtively took off one of his worn Italian loafers and tried on one of the patent leather platform heels. Jerlene looked over at him and said, "Humph!" The whole town knew about Johnny Mack and called him "the peacock" behind his back, but Jerlene didn't come down on Johnny. She had learned at First Delivered True Church that Johnny was loved by Jesus Christ and that no sin was worse than another. She was commanded to love the person, and she had tried to do that regardless.

Some minutes later, a loud and high screech came from the shoe section. Matilda and Jerlene got there quickly and saw Johnny jumping around in one high-heeled platform pump.

"Tildy, what have you done to these shoes!" he shrieked in a high falsetto voice.

"What do you mean, Johnny? What's wrong?" Matilda responded, casting her eye at the small puddle around the shoes and hoping Johnny hadn't urinated there.

Then she saw the dead tadpoles.

"These ... these things!" he screamed. "The shoes are all wet and ... creatures are livin' in 'em!"

He shook the shoe that was near his other foot with his wet rayon sock. Out from the toe end came a squashed dark brown blob before he flung the shoe across the room. Matilda and Jerlene gasped and gazed with wide eyes and open mouths.

"Well, I never in all my life …!" half whispered a bewildered Matilda.

"And just smell *this*!" He thrust a worn tennis shoe in her face. It was barely damp, but it had the distinct scent of roses!

"Can you believe this, Jerlene! Smells like roses around this shoe!" Matilda said.

They looked at each other in bewilderment. The customers that had gathered around the scene now began to chatter and back away. They finally left in their baskets what they had gathered to purchase and went out quickly to spread the word that the ghost had struck one more time.

Nobody had seen a thing suspicious occurring in that area, and upon examination, the other black high-heeled slippers had also been filled with a dead tadpole or two in the toes. The staff members wracked their brains attempting to recall who had worked in that section last—who had replaced the ones sold with ones that had come in. Magnolia said she'd put a few out—some sling-backs and some loafers, but that was all she remembered. Jerlene said that near closing time yesterday some high school girls came in to try on some shoes, but they were all giggling about how one girl's skinny legs looked like Olive Oyl's in a pair of high heels and how another one who tried the same ones made her look like Daisy Duck. They were just acting silly and not bent on mischief, or so it seemed. So it was probable that the mischief had occurred this morning before Johnny came in at lunch time. It was yet another mystery, and nobody knew what to do about it.

# ℅ Chapter 18

The customers that were shopping for Christmas decorations were startled when they heard an unearthly tremolo at the door announcing the arrival of a diva who believed she was operatically talented. She had recently arrived in town from Milwaukee and had told townspeople that she was a descendant of the acclaimed Jenny Lind, the so-called Swedish Nightingale of the nineteenth century. She was a spinster, and she said that her parents had named her Jennifer Lindsay because of the lineage. Since no one could verify this, they let it be. She became a member of the prestigious church in Oak Heights and disseminated the information there. When she was heard singing in the congregation at the church, it was discovered that she had an average voice with a pronounced middle-age vibrato that was too wobbly to blend in, so to her dismay, she was not invited to join the choir.

When she first began to vocalize after moving in, her window was open, and her new neighbors had asked her to please shut up the racket because their basset hound had begun to howl. She became indignant and never spoke to them after that, but Miss Maxie became her great friend, and the two visited regularly. There was at least a thirty-year age difference between the two. They were both collectors, with Miss Lindsay collecting old musical instruments.

One afternoon, Miss Lindsay rang Miss Maxie's doorbell several times to no avail. She pushed the front door, which had not been locked, and found Miss Maxie lying on the living room floor beside the Christmas tree. She had a packet of angel's hair in her hand and had apparently fallen to the floor due to a stroke. Dr. Miller and the coroner determined that this is what had happened. She was smart enough to have made a will that was in the possession of Hortonsville's Lawyer Grant.

Having no relatives, she had bequeathed her property, with all of its furnishings, to Matilda Dayton, with the request that she please set up a display of her best Christmas memorabilia in a room of Tildy's Thrift. She had left $1,000 each to the members of the Harmonettes, and also $1,000 to Jerlene. She bequeathed $500 each to Miss Lindsay, Chester, and Roy. Everyone was very surprised, believing that she had lived in meager circumstances.

When handling her body, the mortician found a tattoo on her upper arm. Knowing that she had been born in Germany, he had ascertained that she had lived there during the period of the Holocaust. In her effects was found a picture of a young woman with the words *mein mutter, Hilda Weiss Komoro,* written on the back. This woman had a dark complexion, and with the picture was found information in German regarding the *Rhineland bastards.*

Research at the library revealed that the term referred to children of African Rhineland-based soldiers from France who intermarried with German women during the World War. These children became Holocaust victims also under Hitler's obsession with racial purity. It was probable that the rest of her family had been casualties of that horror.

Apparently she was from a Protestant family—possibly Lutheran—since she wished her funeral to be held at Crestview Community Church. The whole community came to her service in Oak Heights, a simple one, as was her wish, according to her lawyer; however, holiday garlands and wreaths surrounded her casket.

Pastor Jamison spoke of Miss Maxie's affirmation of resurrection by reading a passage she had underlined in her Bible. It was from Job 19.

## ❦ Eulie Rier Cienfuegos ❧

*For I know my Redeemer liveth,*
*And that He shall stand at the latter day upon the earth.*
*And though my body be destroyed, this I know--*
*That yet in my flesh, I shall see God*
*Whom I shall see for myself and not another.*

She was buried in the cemetery adjacent to the church, the gravesite covered with a manger scene, flowers, and small toys.

\#

Chester and Roy built a small room addition onto Tildy's, and they enlisted the assistance of others in the community. A sign with an arrow pointed to the room that read: Miss Maxie's Christmas Village. Jerlene, Tildy, and the Harmonettes had put up garlands, tinsel, and lights. They also decorated large and small artificial Christmas trees after Tildy's closed. Chester, Roy, and friends had rigged up the toys to move, to speak, and to sing Christmas music. The village was open during the hours of 2–5 p.m. from the day after Thanksgiving through January 6, the day people called Old Christmas, Epiphany, or the Day of the Three Kings.

Sprightly Hector Rios, dressed as one of Santa's helpers, complete with elfin turned-up toes shoes, was hired as the security guard to ensure that no theft or vandalism occurred.

Before the store closed and people got ready for Christmas Eve services at the churches or waited in excitement and/or fatigue for the arrival of Jolly Old Saint Nicholas, Miss Lindsay trooped in, nose in the air, and wearing a long ecru lace gown with a cameo brooch at the neck—a Victorian who had walked off one of the pages of a 1900 Sears Roebuck catalog. Her hair was done up in a large bun with temple tendrils. Behind her came an entourage of well-scrubbed cherubs in white surplices and with big red bows around their necks. Closer inspection showed them to be Horace and Horatio, trying to look serious; the two Higgins boys walking tentatively and looking all around, almost running into the backs of the twins in front of them; the bug twirlers, who walked with a swagger and brows knit to affect a serious demeanor, plus a visiting granddaughter of the Gregorys, who was looking at the floor in front of her as she walked, so as not to have an alien insect attack from the exaggerated account of her grandparents; and another girl who was a newcomer and wore many red and green barrettes in her hair.

As the thirty-odd customers watched in expectancy for whatever was to befall because of Miss Lindsay's appearance with the children, a cart with a large pitcher of water and a box of glasses was rolled in and placed on a white-covered table in front of the children who were lined up behind it. Roy placed a glass before each child and poured water up to the painted line on each.

Miss Lindsay then said in her affected operatic voice, "In honor of this most auspicious of holidays, some of the youth in our community are proud to display their skills by rendering two appropriate tunes for your pleasure. As you can see, their instruments are of fine crystal filled with a water medium to affect the pitches of selections pertinent to the season. Please do enjoy!"

Some of those in the audience looked at each other in confusion, trying to understand what she was saying.

Miss Lindsay gave a tight smile meant to be bright before turning back to the little group for attention as she withdrew eight small mallets with red felt balls at the ends. She placed the mallets beside each glass, knowing she dared not distribute them beforehand lest head bopping and sword fighting should have occurred. Drawing herself up tall and clearing her throat, she held up both hands, a signal for the children to take up their mallets. Then she warbled out, "One, three, five, play!" Three children struck the rims of their glasses, sounding a major chord. The children looked at her for approval. They had been holding their breath until she gave them a tight smile.

The audience clapped. They had finally comprehended the lofty words of introduction from Miss Lindsay.

With looks of relief at the success of this first effort, the group looked at Miss Lindsay, who said, "We will now play 'Joy to the World.' One, two, three, begin!" The children played the tune excellently and then looked up for approval. People clapped, and Miss Lindsay smiled. The bug-twirlers were now feeling comfortable; they elbowed each other and then opened their mouths to chatter. Horace and Horatio had palms in the air, ready to give each other high fives until a withering look from Miss Lindsay brought a halt to all of the levity.

Miss Lindsay said, "And now, let us enjoy 'Jingle Bells'!"

As they played with gusto, the two bug-twirlers decided to click their glasses together in a toast as the group played "Oh!" The two glasses broke, and the other children looked at Miss Lindsay's horrified face under hooded eyelids. The crowd still clapped even though Miss Lindsay looked like she was about to cry. Chester came with a mop, dustpan, and broom as Roy came with the box for the glasses and mallets.

There were handshakes and congratulations all around. There were also smiles and tears for the memory of the eccentric but always cheerful Miss Maxie. Comments were heard suggesting that indeed Miss Lindsay brought back her spirit of Christmas merriment.

# $\mathcal{S}$ Chapter 19

After Christmas, there seemed to be a gray spell. All of the color of the season had disappeared, and the advent of the New Year was dismal as the cold rain came. No one wanted to bundle up and go out, but Tildy's was still open for business, and the enticement to return for patronage was in the window with this prominent sign: Blue Tag Day! Buy One, Get One Free!

When the staff met to think of a way to reduce some of the inventory, Magnolia had said, "I just gave some money in cards for presents. I was too tired to do anything else." That had brought about the decision to entice the community to come in and spend money received as gifts on bargains at Tildy's.

The incident with Johnny Mack and the tadpoles was nearly forgotten, and it seemed that only a few were still afraid that something strange would go on. The store turned into a beehive of activity after the rain let up. Many fittings were taking place at the children's shoe section, on the floor, or with the use of the one straight-backed chair.

The attention of nearly everyone was soon focused on the sound of strident voices from the women's dresses area.

"That my sister's dress. I know it 'cause I was wit' 'er when she bought it. She kept sayin', 'Oh, I love that green silk dress. I jus' love that dress!' We was lookin' to lay her out in it when she died, an' we looked an' looked and couldn't fin' it. That's 'cause somebody done stole it and brung it in here! I'm takin' my sister's dress home! I done saw her green shoes over there too!" Her angry red face held eyes that were bugging out.

"Look! I saw this dress first, and I'm buyin' it for my daughter! They must've made more than one dress!" the incensed brunette screamed.

While the hullabaloo continued, Matilda telephoned the police station, and Chester and Roy came out to try separating the women, who seemed to have superhuman strength.

Annie Mae whispered to Ella next to her, "I knew that girl's sister. Oh, she was a bad un. In that drug house they raided over in Hardcastle. I shore wouldn't want to buy anything of hern. You buy her shoes, and they might take you someplace you don't wanna go. Died real young, she did—'bout twenty-two!"

"So sad!" Ella responded. "Let's get outa here 'fore somebody brings out some kinda weapon!"

They found an opening in the small crowd and ran out to the close scream of sirens. The distraction allowed the fighting women inside just enough time to regain their strength and jerk away from Roy and Chester.

"Gimme 'at dress! Gimme it! Gimme it!" The women pulled at the dress, which finally ripped noisily down the back.

Both stared at it and started screaming again.

"You goan pay for it! You goan pay me!"

"You the one tore it, 'twarnt me!" Hair pulling, fists pummeling, and nail scratching followed.

As the police hustled the bruised, bleeding, and disheveled women out in handcuffs and Roy and Chester helped to disperse the crowd, somebody said, "It's gotten so bad nowadays that folks are even fightin' in little ole thrift stores! You know it must be the end of days!"

# Chapter 20

The wintry days seemed interminable. The heavy snow that came in mid-January appeared to smother the town like a plush blanket that did anything but comfort, because many townspeople became ill with colds and the flu. A few ailing old people died. Among them was Mrs. Penelope Gregory, and Mr. Gregory died within days of her demise. Schools declared snow days and were closed, since few children ventured out with their sniffles and blue noses. A few hardy ones came out to make snow angels, and many wanted to snowball somebody, but there were few potential victims outside, so they went back inside still swathed like cocoons in their heaviest coats and blankets.

Tildy's was closed for two weeks, and Miraculous Sam's old shack burned down from problems with his kerosene heater. First Delivered Church took him in, with the membership rotating his stay at their homes. They hoped he would find salvation.

#

Luna was in bed with the flu and was self-medicating with jars of chicken broth she had frozen in the summer, plus aspirin and spoonfuls of a homey tonic of water, honey, and vinegar.

She was in and out of sleep, daydreaming or in fever, remembering how it felt to be sixteen and so happy in love! She confided in her mother about the ecstasy she was experiencing, and her mother was happy to see her Luna so entranced. She lightly sang a little tune she had created: *I love Troy. He's true blue. Dearest Troy, how I love you.*

They had met in the library after school. He was sitting alone and had the look of a scholar. She liked that. He was wearing a red crewneck sweater with a plaid shirt showing at the collar. His profile was finely chiseled even with his horn rimmed glasses as he read a book and made notes on a pad.

When he stood up from the desk and went over to check the library shelf for another reference, she rose from her table where she too was sitting alone. She said hello to him as she scanned an adjacent shelf. She saw friendly gray eyes and noted his crisp, curly dark hair as he smiled a greeting in response.

"Are you looking for that calculus book Mr. Carr talked about today?"

"Oh! Oh no. I'm not in calculus yet," she flushed. I'm just a junior. You must be in the senior gifted program."

"Well, yes I am," he said. "I'm new here. Name's Troy Dayton from Northern Virginia. Thought I'd brush up before midterm exams."

"I'm Luna Carter. From nowhere but here." She smiled, and he laughed. He had great teeth.

"I'm a junior. We've got some great teachers here. I hope you like them. Does your father work in town?"

"Well, so far they've been great. And yes, Father works all over the town. He's a safety engineer and deals with inspections and compliance issues for a government agency."

The friendship started then. She rehearsed the simple conversation, focusing on the look of his wondrous gray eyes that were fringed with dark lashes. They saw each other in the library often, more by design than otherwise. She was always careful to keep her hands half balled up whenever she took off her gloves. The day came, however, when she was sitting alone and did not notice that he had come up behind her. She had paused to turn a page without her glove and then resumed reading.

"Is that your birthmark, Luna?" he asked, glancing at her hand as he sat down beside her.

She started, then colored a deep purple in shame and embarrassment. "Y-yes," she stammered.

"I'm sorry if I embarrassed you. I surely didn't mean to." He touched her on the cheek. "You have become more important to me than you probably realize. You are such an intelligent, beautiful, and sensitive human being. I would never ever want to hurt you. What I really want to say is that I love you, Luna."

Tears formed in her eyes as she bowed her head. He had moved closer to her and had taken her right hand in his. She was pulling it back slightly, but he held it firmly and said, "I had a best friend in Northern Virginia who was born with a short left leg. He wore a built-up shoe, but he walked with a pronounced limp. A better friend no one could ever find. He was so warm and outgoing. We voted him president of the sophomore class. His family moved away, so we finally lost touch, but everyone really liked him. He was one of a kind, and there was nothing he would not do to help somebody out."

Her dream became troubling, and she tossed restlessly in the bed when she recalled with bitterness what she should have known would happen. She should not have been so naïve; she saw Matilda and Troy together at a table several times, writing in their notebooks and then chatting and smiling at each other. Both were seniors, so she rationalized that they were comparing notes for a senior course.

After exams, there were other scheduled senior activities—picnic, awards night, grad night, and prom. She'd be a part of these exciting events next year as a senior, and she was looking forward to graduating and then being a part of Troy's life forever. She dreamed of their future—their wedding, their travels, the family they would have, and the never-ending love they would share.

He had introduced her to his parents at a Rotary Club luncheon. Mr. and Mrs. Dayton were very charming persons and seemed keenly interested in talking with her, telling her how glad they were that their son had found a nice, intelligent young woman in whom he was apparently quite smitten. He was their only son, and they hoped one day to have little grandchildren to dandle on their knees. Luna had blushed at this and had reflexively put her hand up near her mouth.

Then she woke out of this twilight sleep, feeling nauseous and dizzy, so she went to the bathroom and washed the perspiration from her brow. When she returned to bed, she found that she needed fresh pillow cases and sheets because the bedclothes were wet. She also put on a fresh nightgown and lay down again, feeling weak, and hoping the fever would soon break. She hummed snatches of "In the Gloaming" and soon fell asleep again, hopefully to dream of happier times.

She dreamed of waltzing around with Troy in her beautiful new pink dress at the prom. She and her mom had gone as far as J. Fred Johnson's Department Store in Bristol, Tennessee, to find it. It was a frothy pink frosting of a dress, and with pink lace gloves, Mom's pearl necklace and drop earrings, plus satin shoes dyed pink, she felt sure she would be the belle of the ball. She would tell Troy that a pink and white corsage would complete her ensemble.

All of the girls had been so excited about prom. As she and Troy walked to the library after school before going home, she remembered smiling happily and asking him, "Have you ordered your prom tux yet?"

He had replied, "I haven't definitely made up my mind about what kind to get, or even if I really want to go."

As she lay there between a twilight haze of sleep and awakening, she gave a little moan, remembering what followed.

She had said in astonishment, "But you must go! You're a senior, and it's the senior prom! It will be so memorable for you, especially with the theme 'Forever a Memory.' I've already got my dress. I'm wearing pink." She looked at him expectantly.

"Well, I know you will look great!" He smiled at her but said no more.

*He must be thinking about the cummerbund and tie he'll wear to complement the color of my dress,* she thought.

The prom was Friday, so she had approached him on the Monday prior. "What kind of corsage will you be picking up for me for the prom?"

His face reddened and fell.

"I'll be going with a senior date. That's why I haven't asked you to go with me. I will come back next year for your senior prom if you want me to."

Big tears had welled up in her eyes, and she recalled running toward home. She heard Troy calling out her name, but she continued running toward home, hoping for solace there. Her mother held her and kept trying to console her, to no avail. She tried to stay away from people the rest of that school year after she heard the gossip that Matilda had been Troy's date.

Finally, she woke up from her sickbed and found herself crying again. Matilda had even taken away her first love, and Luna vowed that she would pay for that too.

# Chapter 21

Half-Price Day! Everything was 50 percent off, including the finer garments in the small boutique section that featured a few articles from the gentry of Oak Heights. Some of the after-six soiree clothing with glitz and beading, plus evening clutches and gloves and some fox stoles, were displayed there along with a few men's tuxedoes, bow ties, and dinner jackets. It happened to be on a payday Friday too, so several people were milling about in the shop.

Mattie Jones, a middle-aged buxom matron, was checking out her reflection in front of the floor-length mirror near the doorway of the second room where the women's dresses and skirts were hung. She was admiring herself in a long, green sequined dress she'd tried on in the dressing room as she sucked in her stomach to hide her midriff bulge when an older teenage girl in tight jeans inserted herself in front of her and began to apply lipstick.

"Don't you see me here in front of the mirror?" Mattie said indignantly, raising her voice. Then she muttered, "Got no respect for your elders—got no home training a-tall."

"I was just trying to put on some lipstick, old lady! Dag!" the pimply-faced girl said disdainfully.

"Don't you know where your lips are? Don't need no mirror—they sure are big enough," a teenage boy yelled out among the growing crowd.

"Who said that? I know you're not talkin' to me!"

A string of obscenities streamed from the girl's mouth as she challenged the persons behind her, not knowing just who had made the remark.

A loud argument ensued among the people who began to take sides. Matilda pressed herself into the middle of the crowd to quiet things down. The she yelled, "Jerlene, call the police!"

Jerlene called. Chief Jim Long was eating lunch at the Hot Skillet, so two deputies at the station were dispatched to the fracas. They waded into the mob, trying to sort things out, and finally issued citations to four people for disturbing the peace.

As they were putting the girl into one of the police cars, she yelled out to Matilda, "You gonna regret gettin' me arrested. You better watch your back!"

Deputy Thomas said, "Is that a threat, young lady? You'd better watch your mouth!"

Then Matilda and Jerlene looked at each other and just shook their heads.

"Whew! Well, we know that Satan comes in here looking for bargains too. At least we haven't had any ugly pranks in a while. Roy's doing a good job working as security, and the mirrors high up on the walls must have helped too. Wonder if the person died during that bad flu spell."

Jerlene said, "Maybe somebody read a salvation tract and got convicted."

"Well, whatever stopped it, let's praise the Lord for it!"

"Oh, yes! And you know, the ladies in the back haven't stopped praying since these ugly pranks started happening."

"Annelise said that something good may come out of this, but I certainly don't see how."

"I don't either, but we've got to have faith. It makes all the difference."

# Chapter 22

There were a few days of unseasonably warm weather as the year advanced toward spring. Some crocuses and snowdrops peeped out beside Tildy's, and pastel-colored garments waited in the wings of the shop to replace the displays of Valentine red attire. But on this beautiful day, there were few patrons in the store. Magnolia and Annelise came back from lunch and reported what was happening a block away.

Old Miraculous Sam had come out of hibernation. He'd built another ramshackle place near the railroad station after the fire destroyed his first home. He had two new enterprises going, and a small crowd had gathered at one—his fruit stand where bruised apples, half-dried oranges, and speckled bananas were displayed. As he stood on a wooden crate, he explained that the grocery store had thrown some out, but he announced that the vitamins were still in these better ones, and they could be bought cheaply from him—two for a quarter. At these reduced prices, he announced, everybody in the family could get a piece of healthy fruit.

After he had sold all he could of these, he proved himself to be a holdover from the days of the old snake oil salesmen as he introduced his second enterprise. He took on a morose expression and talked about how his dear departed wife had survived her diabetic leg amputation, but that her death the week following had been due to constipation. Constipation, he felt, was at the root of mankind's physical ills, including cloudy thinking and memory lapses. He told the crowd that he'd spent a lot of time this past winter experimenting and concocting a great boon to mankind, and that he was now willing to share it with the ailing of Hortonville.

"I want to help the community go back to nature and stop puttin' all these chem'cals in they bodies and poisonin' they systems—cloggin' 'em all up."

His display of bottles still bore the labels of Lydia Pinkham, Wine of Cardui, Castoria, Hedacol, and various other brand names. His hand swept in front of them as he said, "Now, this hyar medicine's got a touch of the tribes in it. Y'all know whut I mean. The Cherokee used to be in our area, and more than a few of us'uns done got some of the blood. There's cherry bark tea, black strap molasses, sassafras, pawpaw, a pinch of sulfur, an' a little tetch of turpentine in it. A spoonful of this and a slice of fruit will do the trick! I done give my grandsons a dose to clean them out 'fore spring, and some of them's a-settin' on they pots right now! All of y'all who's ailin' can come and get a free spoonful and chase it with a slice of this here apple I'm goan cut up. Now, if y'all get a little movement and want more, jus' brang a five-doller bill to my new house back of the train station. I got more bottles ready. Y'all know the place. Hit's got a fresh coat of green an' yeller paint."

He had a little bundle of plastic spoons, and as some of the arthritics shuffled up to the stand to take a spoonful, he took out an old knife and cut slices of apple for each person to chase it with. Magnolia and Annelise were incredulous at the sight of yet another one of Miraculous's scams. Their report to Matilda resulted in a call that brought a deputy to the scene. He dispersed the group and cited Miraculous for having no peddler's license.

#

Luna had ventured out on this unseasonably warm day, and standing on the fringe of the crowd, she listened to Miraculous's pitch and watched the little line of people who had been duped into trying a dose. Some of them headed toward Tildy's afterwards. She then imagined the scene that would follow as these people barfed all over Tildy's floor.

*Well, some of these will fix you up, Matilda! Thanks, Sam!*

She continued to walk through the town and headed for the Horton River. She picked up several small flat rocks along the shoreline and skipped them across the calm surface, disturbing some of the water striders.

She crouched and watched the water striders gliding on the placid water. She toyed with the idea of slipping into the water, like a Gollum who had originally emerged from its sludge. *Maybe I don't belong here on the land*, she thought. She stepped into the shallows of the water. The she began to wade in deeper. There was a rustling sound behind her just before she became completely submerged.

"There's something floating in the water!" a female voice yelled out.

Luna's blouse had become snagged on a partially submerged tree branch that had fallen into the water. As the two women went closer, they saw a form and waded out as far as they were able. They finally discerned the shape of a woman. Dragging her out onto the riverbank, Ola Mae recognized her as the woman who had gathered some roses from her front yard. With aging boarders, Ola Mae had found it necessary to learn CPR. Before she administered it, she called out to the other woman, "Magnolia! Call the rescue squad! Quick!"

Magnolia moved with all the alacrity her bumblebee-like bulk could, and the paramedics responded quickly.

# Chapter 23

When she awoke, Luna found herself ensconced in a comfortable clean bed with fluffy blankets and soft down pillows. She was dressed in a long, light muslin gown, embroidered at the wrists. The sun filtered through the white lace curtains, and a soft balmy breeze wafted into the room bringing the sweet fragrance of Ola Mae's flower garden.

"Is this heaven?" she whispered.

Coming through the door at this moment was Ola Mae, carrying a tray of steaming coffee, apple juice, scrambled eggs, grits, a small piece of ham, and a large flaky biscuit with honey and a pat of butter. Utensils rested on a crisp white napkin beside a small yellow rosebud snipped from an early blooming bush.

"Dear child," Ola Mae began, "how are you feeling this morning?"

"All-all right, I guess. What happened?"

"Oh, you just slipped and fell into the river, honey, that's all. But you gonna be all right now."

She smoothed the loose tendrils of hair back from her forehead. "Here, eat something! You'll feel so much better, and it will put more color into your pretty cheeks!"

"Oh," Luna's eyes lightened. "I remember you now. You're the nice lady with the beautiful roses that you let me cut."

"Yes, I'm Ola Mae, and you're here in my home, the Flora Rose. A friend and I went out to pick some watercress along the bank. We call 'em creasy greens, and we cook 'em with some mustard greens and a streak o' lean. It sure tastes good with cornbread and buttermilk. You ever tried some?"

"No, Miss Ola Mae, but it sure sounds tasty!"

She began to eat a piece of the biscuit lathered with butter and honey. As she lifted it up, she remembered that her right hand was exposed, so she started to move it down and toward her. Ola Mae gently stopped her.

"It's okay, honey. I've seen it before," she said gently. "It happens sometimes, but it's just the way it is. Everybody has something different about themselves—some on the inside, and some on the outside, but you're healthy and you're beautiful. We thank God for that!"

Luna felt strangely soothed as she listened to Ola Mae's words. She dared to trust this dark motherly woman and soon ventured to tell her about her life and the pain she had endured as a child. As she talked, her features contorted when she spoke of her long wait to find the one person who was the chief cause of it all.

"Poor child." Ola Mae's eyes misted. "You've suffered, but vengeance and bitterness will not change the past. It's not easy to forgive, but it truly is a choice. You can have a beautiful life if you will make that choice. This is your decision. Do you want a life free of this misery?"

"But I've already found her, and the payback has begun! Soon she will be ruined!" Her jaw tightened.

Ola Mae drew closer to her and said softly, "Tell me how, dear child."

Luna recounted all of the ways she had duped the public into believing Tildy's was haunted and that some type of pestilence awaited those who were patrons there. She said that fewer customers were coming because of fear and that Matilda now had the additional expense of paying a new employee for security purposes. Luna's eyes glittered, and she was almost giddy when she said that Matilda was practically giving things away to entice the public to come in on special sales days. She announced triumphantly that Matilda couldn't keep that up indefinitely and that bankruptcy was sure to follow.

"Did it make you feel better inside as you did these things?" Ola Mae asked.

"No, not really. I felt vindicated until I saw the old customers getting so frightened. They didn't deserve it, and I certainly didn't want any of them to have a stroke or a heart attack over it. Then too, Matilda's workers seemed nice and undeserving of any hurt, but Matilda brought it all on herself and them. It was all her fault!"

Ola Mae waited for a span of time and finally said, "Do you know, dear, that things done in darkness will finally come to light? That's a principle of life, and it is recorded in the scriptures. Jerlene lives here at the Flora Rose, and she enjoys working with Matilda. People change, you know. They very often regret the foolishness of their youth. Children, in particular, can be very cruel to one another. Think on it, dear heart."

Ola Mae held Luna's right hand in hers and knelt beside the bed. Softly and fervently, she took the matter to the Throne of Grace.

# ❦ Chapter 24

Ola Mae told Jerlene that there was a serious situation that had to be rectified, and that prayer for a woman in need of healing of memories and emotions was urgent. Jerlene began to pray and then called the members of the prayer circle at her church. Vilma, Annelise, and Magnolia also happened to be members of the circle.

At the end of the week, Ola Mae and Luna entered Tildy's five minutes before the 4:00 closing hour. Matilda looked up, gave them a friendly smile, and said, "Hello, ladies. I'm sorry, but I'm just closing up. Can you come back tomorrow morning? I open at 9:00."

Ola Mae could faintly feel Luna flinch beside her, but she said to Matilda, "Could we have a little bit of your time for an important personal matter?"

"We?" Matilda looked quizzically at her and the woman beside her.

Luna's hands were hot and clammy as Ola Mae said, "First, I'd like to go and say hello to the girls in the back? Is Jerlene there too?"

"Yes, she's in there with the ladies. Roy and Chester have gone home."

Once in the back room, Ola Mae whispered with urgency, "Come on, ladies; it's prayin' time for two people standin' in the office."

Magnolia began by saying, "Father, we stretch our hands to Thee. No other help we know."

The other ladies joined in fervently, invoking His presence with uplifted hands and Amens as they recalled that where two or three were gathered in His Name, He was in the midst of them. The rays of the evening sun glanced off them through the little window as in blessing.

Through starts and stops interspersed with sobs, Luna confessed that she was the one responsible for the pranks. She told Matilda how she had recalled all of the misery inflicted on her throughout her school days because of her hands. She held them up, now gloveless.

"Yes, I'm Luna Carter, and you bullied and taunted me unmercifully! I can't help the way I was created, but you made fun of me and encouraged the other girls to be hateful and do the same. I had only one friend—just one—and you made both of us suffer," she spat out bitterly.

Matilda's face was blanched and drawn as her tears began to flow. She stammered out, "I've-I've thought of those days, and-and I've regretted it so m-much. I was cruel! C-Can you-you ever forgive m-me?"

"Forgive you? You even took the only man I ever loved and who loved me back regardless of my hands! Just for spite you did that to me!" she cried out, and then she ran out to the side of the building. There she embraced herself, rocking back and forth, and said, "Oh, Mother, how I've needed you!" Sobbingly, she began to sing, "In the gloaming, O, m-my d-darling."

"Luna! Luna! That song!" Matilda ran outside and found her. A little breeze had blown Matilda's hair back from her neckline, and now a russet mark was revealed. It was in the shape of a star—her birthmark.

Luna saw it and gasped. A star! She had been told that her sister had that kind of birthmark!

"You, you've got a st-st-star! Could you be …? No! This is a dream! Could you be Stella? Stella? No, but you're Matilda!"

"Yes, I'm Stella. My name is Matilda Estelle. Matilda was my mother's name. That song you were singing! It was her favorite!

Could you be …? No, it's too much! Could you be my little sister, Selena?"

Breathlessly, she answered, "Yes, but I've always been known by my middle name, Luna."

"Oh, it's a miracle! A miracle! I've finally found my little sister! Thank You! Oh, thank You, God!"

She was crying copiously as she went forward to embrace her, but Selena drew back.

"But you took the only man I've ever loved!" she screamed.

"Yes," Stella said miserably. "I did. I was mean-spirited and selfish. And then—then we fell in love and got married right after graduation. He tried to find a job, but he couldn't, so he joined the Marine Corps and was killed in combat."

She stopped and swallowed the large lump in her throat before continuing.

"I found out that I was pregnant right after he left to go overseas. We had a little daughter, who I named Matilda Selene after you and Mother. He never got a chance to see her. She is now in her second year at law school."

Luna looked incredulous. Stella appeared to have aged ten years within the last hour. Then she continued, "Troy said he had lost touch with you and asked me to please give you a letter from him if I ever saw you again. I have kept it here in my store safe, Let's go inside,"

Once they were there, she walked very slowly towards a large picture on the wall, behind which was her safe. She sighed as she worked the combination, a burden seemingly weighing heavy on her shoulders. Meanwhile, Luna was wondering, *What could he say? And what difference will it make? He forsook me to marry my own sister!*

With trembling hands, Luna took the letter out of the envelope addressed to her. It read:

Dear Luna,

Truly I did love you, and I will always love you. You must be so hurt to know that I am married to someone else. I wanted to be married to you, and I had told my parents that I had met the woman of my dreams and that it was you. But when we were at the Rotary Club luncheon with my parents, they noticed your hands. Oh, they were gracious, but the next day, they called me to tell me there was important business they had to discuss with me. Oh, the business! They said that with your "deformity" (yes, that's what they called it, dear one), they felt that you might pass the gene to their grandchildren so that they too would be malformed, and they didn't want that in the family. They also said they would disinherit me if I went ahead and married you.

So you see, dearest, I had to change plans. I hope you understand. There's a verse of that song you always liked that says it best for me:

In the gloaming, O my darling,
Think not bitterly of me.
Though I passed away in silence,
Left you lonely, set you free.
For my heart was tossed with longing,
What had been could never be.
It was best to leave you thus, dear,
Best for you and best for me.

Always,

Troy

*So! He married my perfect sister instead! And his family and their money were more important than I was! Now I know him for what he really was!* She hurt deep down in the pit of her stomach. Her chest felt as if she would suffocate. She was angry, but relieved to know what had transpired to make him change his mind about her. Stella had forgiven her; now it was her turn to forgive Stella. She knew she had to, and now she wanted to.

"Oh, sister! My sister!" they both cried out as they embraced.

A little later, the ladies in the back room were told that a miracle had happened—that two sisters had been reunited after having been adopted as small children. All of the ladies went home praising God for the miracle and for answered prayer.

# ॐ Chapter 25

It was bound to be the social event of the season! Jay Colby and Darlinda Fields were going to be married! Matilda was heading up the wedding coordination, since it was Jay's parents' corporation that initially financed Tildy's. She felt that anything she could do for that family was never enough, and she was happy to do it. She was ably assisted by Ola Mae, Darlinda's grandmother, and by Jerlene, her best friend.

They had outdone themselves in seeing to the decorations, and the recreation center was lavish in roses and ribbons. Since Jay was a member of Crestview United Church, and Darlinda was a member of New Dawn Community Christian Church, a neutral site had been selected to accommodate the many guests expected for the occasion.

Ola Mae, Matilda, and Jerlene were dressed in pretty pastel colors of mint green, coral, and lavender and were wearing extravagant matching hats for the 2 p.m. event. They sat in the second row of the bride's side. Alisha and Leandro Fields, proud parents of the bride, who had come from Los Angeles, sat with them and were beaming. Barney and Pauline Hardee, stepfather and mother of the groom, were elegantly attired, and their faces were wreathed in happy smiles as they sat on the groom's side with friends.

In the room adjacent to the foyer were matrons of honor Lauranne Sirrah and Wilma Jo Hardee plus four bridesmaids who were friends from the Beantown and Oak Heights communities. They were dressed in yellow lace dresses and carried bouquets of yellow and white baby roses.

Jay looked splendid in his white tuxedo with a yellow rose in the lapel. The best man, handsome Max Hardee, was Jay's uncle, and he was flanked by Lafayette Fields, Darlinda's uncle, and groomsmen who were friends and graduates of the Hortonville Music Conservatory.

Dr. Clemmons, organist of Crestview United, played Handel's *Trumpet Fanfare* magnificently on a wonderful antique organ that had been shipped in with an acoustic shell specifically for the occasion. When the music began, four-year-old Nora Della Sirrah, in a yellow organdy dress, strewed a basket full of yellow and white rose petals gathered from Grandma Ola Mae's front yard. She had a big smile as she almost waltzed down the aisle. Seven-year-old Ben Hardee, adopted son of Barney and Pauline, walked carefully behind her in a white tuxedo as ring bearer.

When all persons were in place, Dr. Clemmons switched to Lohengrin's *Bridal March,* and Darlinda came down the aisle resplendent in a gown encrusted with seed pearls and rhinestones. It was so white that it fairly shimmered with a blue luminescence as she walked. White roses and baby's breath encircled her head above her long shining train.

Matilda and Luna, newfound sisters, sang a duet—*We've Only Just Begun.* No one knew just how meaningful those words were as tears glistened in their eyes.

The Reverend Yram Sirrah, Darlinda's uncle and pastor of New Dawn, performed the ceremony, followed by *The Lord's Prayer,* sung by the Harmonettes's trio, composed of Magnolia, Vilma, and Annelise, all attired in peach satin.

After Mendelssohn's *Wedding March* proclaimed the end of the ceremony, the bridal bouquet was thrown and caught by Violet, who was dressed in glittering purple sequins and teetering around on matching stiletto-heeled shoes. She rushed around waving it in the air and calling out in a frantic high- pitched voice, "Oh, Chester? Chester?"

A little later, under the small twinkling lights of the dance floor pavilion's eaves, Chester was leaning on the hood of his truck and tapping his foot in time to the swinging music of Lafayette's jazz band as the couples inside danced the night away.

# ❧ Epilogue

The principal of Hortonville High School had announced his resignation, effective the first of the incoming calendar year, due to serious illness, and the new one was coming by train today. All school principals in the county had traditionally been male, but this one was a female, Dr. C. J. Friedman.

The record of her distinguished accomplishments had been cited in the *Hortonville Gazette,* and the community was sure she would be the one to improve test scores, promote greater parental involvement, and foster high standards for students, faculty members, and staff.

There were scattered conversations going on at Tildy's this Wednesday morning. One of these was about the new principal's surname: Friedman.

"I believe her name is German, and she just might be Jewish. I've met some Jews named 'Fried' when I was stationed in Frankfurt," a balding gray-bearded man was telling some other men at the dress shirts section.

"We ever had a Jewish principal here?"

"No, not that we ever asked one what he was. You think there might be a problem?"

"Wal, mebbe the kids won't be able to say 'Merry Christmas' anymore! I don't like it!"

"Never can tell. There's lots of Christian Jews now, I hear."

"Wasn't Jesus Christ a Jew?"

"Oh, naw, He was a Nazarene. They's diffrunt!"

"Did you know that they've got horns? I saw some on a statue of Moses in a 'cyclopedia!"

Somebody gave a loud laugh.

"That was supposed to show the spokes of brightness that came from Moses when he came down from Mt. Sinai with the Ten Commandments! Jews don't have horns!"

"Well, they wears these little caps, and I'm a gonna ask 'em what they hidin' under there nex' time I see one!"

#

The little group was excited. Representatives from the chamber of commerce and the school board were at the train station to welcome the new principal of Hortonville High School, who was to arrive at 2:00 p.m. It was decided that the president of the board would be the first to speak words of welcome to Dr. C. J. Friedman.

When the train came to a stop and the porter stepped off to assist passengers, a small salt and pepper-haired middle-aged woman in a tan suit alighted from the steps of the train. The energetic and smiling group moved toward her in welcome.

"Dr. Friedman, welcome to Hortonville," Morris Macon, school board president, said, stepping forward with a smile and extending his hand.

"Oh, you are mistaken, sir," the woman said in a tremulous voice. "My name is Mary Bates, and my grandson is supposed to be here to pick me up." She craned her neck, scanning the area.

A dark-skinned middle-aged woman stepped off the train next. She wore a gray cloche hat and a fashionable navy blue suit with gray suede shoes and handbag. She also carried an expensive leather briefcase.

"Are you here to meet me? I'm Dr. C. J. Freeman." She smiled and extended her hand. "I noticed in the newspaper I read on the train that my name had been misspelled."

Mr. Macon's face blanched, but he regained his composure, shook her hand, and welcomed her to Hortonville. The rest of the group had exchanged glances and looked somewhat discomfited. They had not been prepared to meet a woman of color, but they attempted to cover their perturbation and began to greet her.

After pleasantries had been exchanged, she was driven to the school and escorted to her new office. At the door, she reflected on the fact that she had never been sent to the principal's office, but now she was going into this one in a role she would never have expected when she was enrolled here. Funny how everyone focused on her university days and following. They didn't know that she had been enrolled at Hortonville High School for two years before her family moved to the District of Columbia area.

The smell of new leather greeted her. A plush office chair was situated behind a beautifully polished mahogany desk, on which was placed a lovely fruit bowl. It was all very nice. *Now who is going to expect special perks for all of this?* she wondered. *Well, maybe they won't expect anything. I will be a gracious receiver, express my appreciation, and give my benefactor the benefit of the doubt.*

On the train, she had already begun a to-do list. She took it out and placed it on the desk. At the top was the heading **Cora Jane's Priorities**. Last on the list, but not least, was the underlined entry: *Find Luna*.